LT
F

MEI

MEIER, SUSAN

MILLIONAIRE DAD, NANNY NEEDED!

DATE DUE

MILLIONAIRE DAD, NANNY NEEDED!

MILLIONAIRE DAD, NANNY NEEDED!

SUSAN MEIER

THORNDIKE
CHIVERS

This Large Print edition is published by Thorndike Press, Waterville, Maine, USA and by BBC Audiobooks Ltd, Bath, England.
Thorndike Press, a part of Gale, Cengage Learning.

The text of this Large Print edition is unabridged.
Other aspects of the book may vary from the original edition.
Set in 16 pt. Plantin.
Printed on permanent paper.

LIBRARY OF CONGRESS CATALOGING-IN-PUBLICATION DATA

Meier, Susan.
    Millionaire dad, nanny needed / by Susan Meier. — Large print ed.
        p. cm. — (Thorndike Press large print clean reads) (The wedding planners ; 5)
    Originally published: New York: Harlequin, 2008.
    ISBN-13: 978-1-4104-0969-0 (alk. paper)
    ISBN-10: 1-4104-0969-4 (alk. paper)
    1. Weddings—Planning—Fiction. 2. Large type books. I. Title.
PS3563.E3463M55 2009
813'.54—dc22   2008043967

BRITISH LIBRARY CATALOGUING-IN-PUBLICATION DATA AVAILABLE

Published in 2009 in the U.S. by arrangement with Harlequin Books, S.A.
Published in 2009 in the U.K. by arrangement with Harlequin Enterprises II B.V.

U.K. Hardcover: 978 1 408 41249 7 (Chivers Large Print)
U.K. Softcover: 978 1 408 41250 3 (Camden Large Print)

Printed in the United States of America
1 2 3 4 5 6 7 13 12 11 10 09

Thanks to all the Ladies of Wedding Belles
for a fun experience writing this continuity
and special thanks to Kim, Lydia and Suzy,
the editors of my book for their help and insight.

Audra is the accountant at The Wedding Belles and has some great tips on sticking to a wedding budget, no matter how big or small:

- Create a budget. Determine the amount of money you have to spend and apportion it appropriately. Figure out how much you can afford to spend on your dress, the decorations, the caterer . . . and everything else needed to make your day perfect. Don't forget the little things, like paying the singers and clergy at the ceremony.

- Don't stop with a budget! Once you determine how much you have to spend, keep track of your real expenditures on a spreadsheet. Review the sheet regularly to have a clear picture of where your money is going and how much you have left to spend.

- Bargain shop. Wedding shops frequently run sales on bridal gowns. There are places on the Internet to purchase inexpensive invitations. Rather than buy from the first shop, do a little investigating, and you may just find exactly what you want at a lower price.

Chapter One

The Wedding Belles' three-story townhouse in the heart of Boston was always a flurry of activity, but that Friday, the number of people and the noise level they created had hit new heights. Brides — accompanied by their attendants and clucking mothers — filled the offices and spilled into the hall-ways. The scent of chocolate cake wafted through the air. A rainbow of color flowed from gowns through flower arrangements and favors for the reception dinner tables. Sequins on white bride dresses and veils caught the morning sun pouring in through the windows and sent flashes of light through the foyer, into the corridors, up the stairs.

Audra Greene, accountant for Wedding Belles, worked her way through a gaggle of giggling bridesmaids, creating a rustle of satin and lace. She edged around the wedding party considering various shades of blue and the party trying on dresses in pinks and lavenders, smiling politely and saying, "Hello," and "Excuse me," on her way to her third-floor office.

Finally there, she closed the thick wooden door and leaned against it with a sigh.

The Belles' copper-haired, pixie-featured general assistant, Julie Montgomery, laughed. "It's a jungle out there."

Removing her navy blue coat, Audra strode to her antique desk. "How many weddings are they working on?"

"Let's see. The weddings for June of next year are in the initial planning stages. September brides are finalizing details."

"And April brides are panicking?" Audra hung her coat in the closet before she slid onto her tall-backed brown suede chair in front of the billowing yellow silk drapes that gave the room the rich, elegant feel that she loved.

Julie tilted her head, considering that. "The Belles like to think of it as maximizing last-minute opportunities." With a chuckle, she went back to inputting invoices into the computer to pay that month's bills.

Audra's chest tightened as she watched Julie. The assistant — and the Belles for that matter — had no reason to check into the most recent deposit in the business account and discover it was actually every cent of Audra's savings. Or that the estimated income taxes they'd sent in wouldn't cover this year's bill. Paying the difference would drain the Wedding Belles' coffers and they wouldn't have enough money for the wedding they'd promised to Julie. But Audra knew.

Still, she didn't immediately turn on her computer and begin writing the e-mail to the other Belles about their dire financial straits. She needed to tell them — this morning — before Julie's wedding plans went any further. But she couldn't do it in front of Julie.

"Julie, would you do me a favor?"

Always eager to please, Julie quickly glanced up. "Sure."

"I should have grabbed a bottle of water from the kitchen, but I have something I have to do right now. It can't wait —" Loath to ask the Belles' assistant to run this kind of personal errand, Audra had no choice. She needed a few minutes of privacy, and when Julie entered invoices for payment she shared Audra's office. "Could you get me a bottle of water?"

"Sure!"

Julie sprang from her seat. "I can't believe you'd hesitate to ask me! I'm so indebted to you guys. I'd do anything for any of you."

At the gratitude and affection she heard in Julie's voice, Audra winced. "Please, you don't need to say that."

Julie smiled radiantly, her pretty blue eyes shining. "Are you nuts? That's like saying I shouldn't be grateful! There isn't enough gratitude in the world to show you how much I appreciate what you're doing for me."

Disappointment tightened Audra's chest, squeezing her heart. Julie was the kindest, most unselfish person Audra knew and life had treated her abysmally. The Belles weren't paying for her wedding because *they* were wonderful. They had made the decision because Julie was wonderful. Sweet. And she deserved the kindness. Audra felt as if she, personally, were the one letting her down. After all, she was the one in charge of finances.

At the office door, Julie turned with a smile. "I'll be back in a second."

Heartsick, Audra said, "Take your time."

Julie left the room, and Audra sank into her chair, turned on her computer and was about to begin composing the e-mail to the Belles explaining that they couldn't afford to pick up the tab for Julie's wedding. But with Julie's appreciation still hanging in the air, she couldn't do it. The words simply wouldn't come. The most she could write was a request for an emergency meeting in the conference room. She hit Send, then shifted over to a word-processing program to try to compose a few lines she could say in the meeting to tell the Belles they couldn't afford Julie's wedding.

Once again, she couldn't think of a way to soften the blow of having to break a promise. So, instead of typing on her keyboard, Audra reached for her phone and tapped out the numbers for her mother's cell phone.

"Are you busy?"

"Always," her mother said with a laugh. "But you never call me at work, so you must have a problem that's more important than the blueberry pies I'm baking."

"I do."

"What's up?"

Worried that Julie would return in the middle of her story, Audra said, "I don't have time to explain, but we're out of money."

Her mother gasped. "Wedding Belles is going bankrupt?"

"No, we have enough money to make it through the next few months if we're careful. The problem is we promised our assistant a wedding. If we give her the wedding we've been planning, we'll end up over our heads in debt. If we don't, we have to go back on our word."

"Oh, honey. That's terrible."

Audra glanced at the door. "I shouldn't have called. Julie's going to be back any second and I can't talk in front of her. But I feel awful and I don't know what to do. I can't even think of a way to explain our problem in an e-mail to the Belles. I'm a mess!"

"Wow, for you to admit you can't organize or plan yourself out of a situation, things must be bad. Dominic's gone," she said referring to Dominic Manelli, the youngest of the Manelli children, current CEO of Manelli Holdings, only resident of the family home and Mary Greene's employer. "Left as if his feet were on fire. So why don't you come over? I'll make coffee. We'll talk. Two heads are always better than one. Maybe together we could come up with something?"

The prospect of getting out of the office relieved some of Audra's stress. Even *thinking* about staying in the same room with Julie while she entered invoices and chatted happily about her wedding sent a dagger through Audra's heart. And her mother was

12

smart. Analytical. That's where Audra had gotten her own logical thinking ability. Maybe together they could figure a solution to this problem? Or if nothing else, maybe they could find a way to soften the blow, not just for Julie, but for the Belles who would be devastated at not being able to keep their promise.

"I'll be over in about twenty minutes."

"I should have pie for you by then."

Audra laughed. Her mother always knew how to make her feel better. "Just make a crust and lots of chocolate pudding."

Her mother chuckled. "Should I have whipped topping?"

"Yes!" She sighed. "Thanks, Mom."

Audra hung up the phone and rose from her seat just as Julie entered the room. "Here's your water."

"Thanks." Audra set the bottle on her desk, then pulled her practical coat from the closet and shrugged into it. "I need to go out. I'll be gone for most of the morning. If anybody's looking for me, they can reach me on my cell."

Looking a bit perplexed, Julie said, "Okay."

Audra slipped out of the office. In the corridors and on the stairs, she once again battled brides, bridesmaids and sparkly gowns to get to the door and out into the fat fluffy flakes falling on Boston.

Traffic prevented her from making it to the Manelli estate in twenty minutes as she'd hoped. Almost forty minutes had passed before the guard at the gate let her onto the property. The heavy snow that had been falling steadily clung to the lush evergreens that lined the long lane and the bare branches of stately oaks in the front yard, making the Manelli estate a winter wonderland. Audra drove around the circular driveway to the servants' entrance, and was surprised to find a pretty blue Mercedes parked in front of the kitchen door.

Getting out of her car, she noticed a man dipping into the backseat of the car. Dressed in a black suit and topcoat with a white scarf around his neck, he looked as if he could have stepped off the cover of a magazine. Except, when he pulled out of the car again, he was wrestling a baby, a diaper bag and a bottle.

The baby, a boy if the blue snowsuit was any indicator, wiggled out of the extra blanket wrapped around him. It landed in a puddle in the driveway. Then the bottle fell. Then the diaper bag. Even the baby slipped a bit.

"Damn it!"

Audra ran over. "Here," she said, stooping down to gather the soaked blanket, bottle and diaper bag.

"Thanks."

Recognizing the voice, Audra snapped her gaze upward. "Dominic?"

He looked down. "Yes?"

Baby items in hand, she rose. She'd last seen Dominic Manelli when she was twelve, attending her final Manelli employee Christmas party with her mother. That would have been fourteen years ago. The teenage Dominic she remembered from her childhood had grown into a tall, lean man. His black hair was as short as he could possibly wear it, making his wide brown eyes his most prominent feature. His once boyish grin was now a sexy smile.

"It's me. Audra Greene. Mary's daughter."

"Oh, my goodness! Audra!" His gaze rippled from her blond hair, down her simple coat. "Wow. Look at you. All grown-up."

"Yep." She laughed, but having Dominic notice her as a woman made her tummy flip-flop. She'd had a monster crush on him most of her childhood. "Time didn't stop just because my mother wished it would."

Dominic chuckled, juggling the baby, who appeared to be about six months old. Wisps of yellow hair peeked out from the pale blue hood of a one-piece snowsuit. Curious blue eyes studied Audra.

"Whoever decided babies' winter wear should be made of slippery material needs to be shot." He jostled the baby again. "I'll never get used to holding him!"

Audra didn't know Dominic had gotten married, let alone that he'd had a child, but her mother didn't talk about the family she worked for. That was one of the reasons the Manellis loved and trusted her . . . and had promoted her over the years from cook all the way to household manager.

"Your baby looks about six months old. If you're not accustomed to holding him by now, you're in trouble."

"He's not mine." He sucked in a breath. "Well, he is now. Joshua is my brother Peter's son."

Audra nearly groaned at her stupidity. It had been all over the papers three months ago when Dominic's brother, Peter, and his wife had been killed when their private plane went down in a wooded area in New York. "Oh, Dominic. I'm so sorry."

"It's all right."

"No, it's not. I should have realized this was Peter's son." To shift the conversation from the painful topic, Audra hoisted the diaper bag over her shoulder and opened her arms to the baby. "Let me take him while you get the rest of his things out of your car."

Dominic unexpectedly laughed. "I'd let you take him, but I can't get the rest of his things out of the car. I don't even know how they installed the car seat. Forget about figuring out how to take it out. And I have to take it out. I'll be using the SUV for him from now on. I should have thought that through before taking this car to pick him up."

"You want the car seat out?"

"Yes."

"I'll get it." With a smile, she handed him Joshua's bottle and slid the diaper bag up his arm onto his shoulder. "I have four nieces and nephews. If I want to take them for ice cream I have to be able to get all their seats out of my sisters' cars and into mine."

"Wouldn't it be simpler just to take your sister's car?"

She frowned. "I have two sisters. I can't drive two cars at once. I have to take the seats out of one of them."

He chuckled again. "I forgot what a stickler for detail you are."

She made a face at him, then ducked into

the back seat of his Mercedes, inspecting for the belts and clasps that secured the seat. "After all the fun we had slipping out of your family's employee Christmas parties, how could you forget me?"

"I didn't forget *you*. I said I forgot what a stickler for detail you are. And, if I remember correctly, *we* didn't slip out of my family's Christmas parties. *I* slipped out. You always found me and squealed on me."

"I was twelve. To me that was fun."

"Right."

"Bet you were glad when I stopped coming with my mom."

"About the time you stopped coming I stopped slipping out." He laughed. "It seems that as I got older, the parties got less boring."

Bent inside the car, Audra called, "Really?"

Dominic took a pace back. She probably didn't realize she was presenting a very enticing view of her backside, and as a gentleman appreciative of the help she was giving him, Dominic diverted his attention.

"Yes. When I became the administrator of the Manelli College Scholarship, as my first full-fledged family responsibility, I thought it was best to begin getting to know the people in line for the money so I could choose the right recipient."

"I never did thank you."

Her voice drew his gaze back to his car where she busily worked on freeing the baby seat. This time he noticed the long length of leg exposed beneath her coat. She certainly wasn't twelve anymore. And from the way she didn't hesitate to help him, she'd become a lot like her generous, happy mother. He couldn't believe he'd thought her annoying all those years ago when she'd always found his Christmas party hiding place and gone running to his dad.

"Why would you want to thank me?"

"For the scholarship."

"You earned it."

She pulled out of the car, then reached in and retrieved the car seat. "All set."

"Thanks."

"You're welcome." She motioned to the kitchen door. "I'll just follow you in. We'll give the car seat to my mom and have her assign someone to put it in your SUV."

Dominic said, "Great." He started toward the door, but the diaper bag strap slipped off his shoulder and landed with a thump on his forearm. That caused the bottle to fall. The already-wet baby blanket billowed beside the bottle and even the baby looked precarious.

"Damn it."

Joshua began to cry and Audra grimaced. Obviously feeling sorry for him, she reached for the little blue bundle of joy. "I'll take the baby. You put the bottle in that side compartment on the diaper bag. Then put the diaper bag in the car seat and the wet blanket behind the diaper bag and then carry the car seat."

Dominic handed Joshua to her. "I swear I will learn how to do this stuff."

Baby on her arm, she headed for the door again. "Of course you will. All new parents need a little time."

Reminded of his brother and sister-in-law and how silly they'd been, fussing over Joshua in the first days after his birth, Dominic sucked in a breath to control a burst of sadness, as he shoved the bottle into the diaper bag.

"Yeah. Well, if there's one thing I don't have, it's time. When Marsha's mother discovered she had cancer and the doctors recommended she begin chemotherapy immediately, I had to take Joshua. Now. Today. I don't have a nanny, so I'll be walking the floor with him tonight. Without a clue of what I'm doing."

Almost at the door, she glanced over her

shoulder at Dominic. Her pretty eyes filled with concern that she quickly masked with a big smile before she said, "You'll do great."

Joshua dropped his rattle and without a second's hesitation, she dipped, scooped it up and tucked it in her coat pocket — not giving the dirty rattle back to Joshua — and without missing a beat in the conversation.

"Waiting for my sisters to come home, I've walked the floor. At two o'clock in the morning it seems like hell, but then you cuddle the baby against you and whisper sweet things, and he settles down. You'll feel like a million dollars because you could soothe him."

Tucking the diaper bag into the car seat, Dominic stood in awe. She didn't merely know what to do. She knew what not to do, and both appeared to be second nature to her.

"I'd give you just about anything you wanted if you'd help me tonight."

Audra laughed.

"I'm serious." He took a breath and glanced at the baby in her arms who was no longer crying but appeared very happy nestled against her chest. Dominic studied the calm baby and the woman holding him for only a second before he said, "Except, I'd want more than one night's help. If you could spend the next month with me while I interview nannies, I'd make it worth your while."

She winced. "Sorry. No can do. I have a job."

"I know you have a job. I paid for you to get your degree, remember? I'm not asking you to help me forever. Just the three or four weeks that I'll need to interview nannies."

When she opened her mouth to argue, he cut her off, saying, "Look, I'm smart enough to recognize when I'm in over my head and smart enough to recognize a person well qualified to get me out. Plus, you're from a family I know. I can trust you. If we need to juggle a few things, I'm in the right circles and have enough clout that no matter who employs you, I can arrange for you to get the time off."

She reached for the knob on the back door. "Even if you could arrange it, I can't take time off right now. I have a big money problem that I have to solve. That's why I'm here. My mom volunteered to talk me through it."

"You have a money problem?" Standing in his snow covered driveway in front of the huge Tudor-style mansion that had been in his family for generations, he motioned in a circle with his hand. "Look around. The one problem I don't have is money." A few quick strides brought him beside her. "If you need money, I'm your guy. Didn't I just say I'd pay you handsomely?"

"My problem's too big to be covered by the salary of someone you'd hire to be a nanny for a few weeks."

"How much money would you need to get out of trouble?"

She sighed. "Dominic, it's too much —"

"Nothing is too much." He nodded at Joshua. "He's my family. For Manellis, money is no object when it comes to family."

She laughed and shook her head. "You can't pay me a hundred thousand dollars for a little bit of work."

"Why not?"

"Because it's illogical."

"Not really. The way I see this, it will probably take me a month to find a nanny. So you're giving up a good bit of time. And I've already told you money's no object. Not because I don't know the value of a dollar but because Joshua's that important to me. You have the expertise I need but no money. I have money but need your expertise. To me it's a perfect fit."

She drew a breath. "Dominic —"

"Please?"

"I can't take a month off work."

"You can go to work. I really only need help at nights anyway."

"Right. Who's going to watch Joshua during the day?"

"I was hoping your mom could," he said, his lips lifting into a sheepish smile. "I know it's not in her job description, but I don't think she'll turn me down. Especially since she's got plenty of staff she can assign to take turns with him. But that still leaves me with nights —" He paused, caught the gaze of Audra's pretty blue eyes and held it. "Please."

"I don't know —"

"I *do* know. I know your family. It's in your blood to help people." Which was why he persisted. Her mother could never resist a person in need, but her mother was also the head of his household. Though she had staff, she and everybody on her staff worked set hours. He might be able to temporarily squeeze Joshua into their schedules during the day, but he couldn't press them for night duty, too. And he most desperately needed someone for night duty. Not for himself but for the poor baby entrusted to his care. "Think of Joshua."

She glanced at the baby in her arms.

Wonderful Joshua picked that precise second to grin toothlessly at her. She groaned. Joshua was getting to her.

"I'll give you fifty thousand dollars up front and fifty at end of the month. If it goes longer, I'll pay you twenty-five thousand a week." Holding her gaze steadily, he said, "Money's never been an object for me. You need money, and Joshua needs you."

CHAPTER TWO

They stepped into the enormous working kitchen of the Manelli mansion. Audra's mom turned from the stainless-steel stove. As always her short brown hair and simple black dress were neat as a pin, and her blue eyes sparkled. Her gaze touched on Dominic then Audra then Joshua.

"I thought you were coming here to chat with me," she said, shifting from the stove to one of three islands with beige-and-gold-flecked black granite countertops that sat on functional beige ceramic tile floors.

"We met in the driveway."

"And found a baby under the big oak by the garage?"

"This is Peter's son, Mary," Dominic said. "I got a call from Marsha's mom this morning. She's ill and can't raise Joshua as she'd wanted. We all agreed the smartest thing to do was have me take over."

"Oh, Dominic, I'm so sorry," Mary said,

walking to them. "But this actually might work out better for Joshua."

"Yeah," Dominic chided. "He's much better off in the hands of a guy with absolutely no baby experience."

"You'll get the hang of being a daddy," Mary said, reaching for the baby. "And this baby needs to know his dad's family, as well as his mom's."

Audra handed the squirming little boy to her mother, and he immediately began to cry.

"Oh-oh." Mary chuckled, and then brushed her lips across the baby's forehead. "Somebody's sleepy."

She made a move to hand him to Dominic, but Audra took him. She wasn't ready to explain to her mother that she'd agreed to help Dominic for the next month, and decided that was Dominic's job, anyway. She faced Dominic. "Do you have a crib ready for him to sleep?"

"Damn it!" He ran his hand over the top of his head in frustration. "No."

"It's okay." She laid crying Joshua across her arm and began to rock him. "Did Marsha's mom give you a baby carrier by any chance?"

"Yes."

"He's small enough that he can nap in

that. Where is it?"

"In the trunk with two duffel bags of baby clothes and what seems like a hundred stuffed animals that Marsha's mom said he couldn't live without."

"Mom, can you rock him while we bring those things inside?"

Her mother gave her an odd look, but smiled and said, "Sure," as she took Joshua again. "Come on, little sweetie-pie. Aunt Mary will take off all these heavy clothes and tell you a story."

Audra's mom left the kitchen, and Audra and Dominic stepped out into the fat white snowflakes again. "So, I'm guessing you want me to tell your mom about our arrangement."

"She's your employee, not mine. Besides, you're the one making her watch a baby for the next few weeks until you hire a real nanny. The honor falls to you."

He laughed. "I just didn't want to step on any toes."

"When you tell her you're paying me well to work nights for you, my mom won't bat an eye. If there's one thing she understands, it's not going into debt when someone's offering you money. It wasn't easy raising three girls with no husband. She knows a smart person doesn't turn down a good opportunity. I've already told her that Wedding Belles is in a bit of a financial bind." She shrugged. "She'll probably be proud of me."

He chuckled again as he opened the trunk of his car, revealing two duffel bags, a baby carrier and at least twenty stuffed animals. "These are the toys and clothes Marsha's mom said Joshua can't do without. I'll be getting the rest of his things this afternoon."

"You don't have somebody you can send to get them?"

He shrugged and bent into the trunk to gather the stuffed animals. As he handed an armload to Audra, he said, "It doesn't seem right to send someone. Marsha's mom is family. And she's sick. I think it's better for me to do it personally."

She smiled. What a softie he was. "Yeah."

Dominic hoisted the two duffel bags out and nodded to the back entrance. "You open the door for me. We'll dump these in the kitchen and come out and get the rest."

Leading the way, Audra said, "I think we should leave Joshua with my mom this morning, drive to Marsha's mom's for the remainder of the baby things and then hit a furniture store."

"For a crib?"

"And high chair. Changing table. Dress-

29

ers. Toy box." She grinned at him. Having always had to watch her pennies, even talking about spending somebody else's money was fun. Especially when he had so much. "Then we can go to a department store and get a swing, play yard, baby tub."

He rolled his eyes. "Nothing else?"

"I thought money was no object."

"Money might not be an object, but time is. I had four important meetings scheduled for this morning."

Audra opened the kitchen door and walked to the first of the three islands in the huge room. She set the stuffed animals on it. "If you don't mind risking my taste in baby furniture, I could do those things for you. I already told our assistant, Julie, that I'd be out most of the morning."

His dark eyes brightened with hope. "I wouldn't care if you bought a purple crib."

Audra laughed. "Actually you would. But I'm thinking more in the line of white furniture." Familiar with the Manelli home, she added, "I'll need a suite of rooms for Joshua and his nanny. The nanny's room can probably stay furnished as it already is. The sitting room will probably be good as is, too. But one bedroom of the suite should be emptied so I can set up the nursery."

"I think I have just the suite. Come with me."

As Dominic walked Audra through three long corridors to the opulent entrance hall that led to the stairway, memories flooded her. Every time she'd been in this house, the carved wood banister of the wide circular stairway had been decorated with red velvet bows and twinkling white lights. A ten-foot fir dressed with silver stars and gold ornaments had always filled the foyer.

But as they ascended the stairs, the strongest of Audra's memories were of scrambling around, opening doors, going into rooms typically off-limits to the guests, trying to find Dominic's hiding place. She was twelve when she stopped attending the Manelli Christmas parties with her mom. That was the year she'd realized she wasn't looking for Dominic to rat him out to his dad but because she liked him and she hated being a cliché. The cook's daughter who swooned over the son of her mom's wealthy employer? No way. She intended to be a success in her own right, find a man who would swoon over her, and be somebody herself.

If only she'd stuck to that plan.

At the top of the stairway, Dominic said, "This way," pressing his hand at the small of her back to direct her down the hall to the right.

Audra smiled and nodded, but tingles of awareness formed on her back where his hand rested. Another woman might have been alarmed at the attraction, worried about picking up her crush right where she'd left off when she was twelve, but Audra knew she had no reason for concern. Only this time it wasn't because she refused to be a cliché. Adult Audra was smart enough to stay away from Dominic because he was a playboy.

That much of his story her mother had told. Not by way of gossip, but through offhand comments. She'd refer to Dominic as flirty Dominic. Or say she had only the senior Manellis to cook for because Dominic was in Monaco or Vegas or with friends again. Or when forced to work a weekend, she'd frequently say that Dominic had charmed her into cooking for yet another party for his friends.

That was why Audra had been so surprised to see him in the driveway with a baby. Not because she hadn't heard that he'd married or had a child, but because subconsciously she'd never expected him to settle down. Dominic might have taken over the serious job of running his family's conglomerate, but a playboy leopard like that couldn't change his lifestyle spots.

And she knew all about those spots. Her fiancé, a supposed "reformed" playboy, had left her at the altar. He'd humiliated her in front of her friends and family. And when he finally did call to explain, he'd blamed it all on her. She was too strong. He was afraid that if he tried to tell her that he didn't want to marry her, she wouldn't hear him out. She wouldn't argue or discuss. She'd simply demand he be at the church. The only way he'd believed he could stop their wedding was to not show up.

Audra swallowed, willing away the sense of failure that caused her breath to freeze in her chest. That had been almost a year ago. She hadn't even thought about it in months. But right at this moment, standing by a man very similar to the man who had dumped her, it felt like yesterday. The warmth of humiliation washed through her. As if it wasn't bad enough he'd embarrassed her, he'd all but told her she was a total zero as a woman as well. A bossy, nagging harpy.

Thanks, David.

Yeah. She was perfectly safe with Dominic Manelli.

Dominic removed his hand as they walked

into the group of rooms that had been his before he'd taken over the master suite. He couldn't believe the zing of attraction he'd gotten when he set his palm on Audra's back to direct her down the hall, but it shouldn't have surprised him.

Though the Audra he remembered was a short, chubby cherub with big blue eyes and a riot of yellow curls, she'd grown into a beautiful woman. Tall and slender with sleek, sophisticated golden hair and blue eyes that were both warm and sexy, Audra would turn any man's head.

"This is the sitting room."

A few steps in front of him, Audra appraised the overstuffed sofa and chair, coffee table, armoire and bar in the corner with a frown.

"It's not supposed to be huge. It's just a sitting room."

She faced him. "It's okay. I was simply thinking it needs a rocker and maybe a TV."

He hit a switch, and the armoire doors opened. "TV, CD player, DVD player. The works."

"Great. I'll get a rocker at the furniture store, and this room will be perfect for a nanny's needs."

He pointed at two white doors on the wall to the right. "That was my bedroom. And that," he said, motioning to the second door, "leads to a room I used for storage. It's empty now, so it's all ready for baby furniture."

"Is there a door that connects the two rooms?"

"No."

"We'll need one."

"Talk to your mom. She takes care of the house. If there's anything you need to have fixed, remodeled or repaired, she does the hiring."

"Got it." She nodded and turned away from him, still appraising.

Feeling safe, Dominic let his gaze ripple from her tiny waist, down her backside to her shapely legs. The part of him that longed to forget his responsibilities and flirt with her begged to be given at least a few seconds of consideration, but he silenced it. He had to get her set up, rush with her to Marsha's mom's, then hurry to the office. He didn't have time to slowdown the process. He honestly wondered if he'd ever get another free minute. Running the monolithic family business was overwhelming all by itself, but as of an hour ago he had also become a daddy.

A daddy.

"Give me another second to check out the

empty room."

Glad she knew what she was doing, Dominic said, "Sure. Knock yourself out."

Audra disappeared into the storage room, and he blew his breath out on a tired sigh. The second he'd taken Joshua from Olivia Trabold's arms, memories began tripping over themselves inside his head. Peter talking incessantly about becoming a dad. Agonized Peter suffering with Marsha as they tried unsuccessfully for nearly ten years to create a child. Peter passing out cigars in the hospital waiting room, so proud of his brand-new son that his smile had lasted a week.

And Dominic standing behind him, making faces at his sap of a brother. Dominic didn't deserve to be Joshua's father. The baby should have known strong, wonderful Peter. Not crazy, party guy Dominic.

Audra walked out of the empty room. "As soon as we install a door that connects the two bedrooms, this will be perfect. Let's go see how my mom is making out with Joshua."

Dominic followed her down the back stairs to Mary's office. They entered to find her sitting in her tall-backed chair behind her desk with Joshua nestled against her.

Audra sighed. "Look how cute!"

"I know. I'm an adorable grandmother."

Audra laughed. "I was talking about Joshua. He's so beautiful."

Dominic puffed with pride as if he'd had something to do with the little boy's appearance into this world, but he stopped himself. This was Peter's son. The child for whom Peter had yearned for a decade. Dominic felt like an interloper, a thief who'd usurped his brother's job and his child, who wasn't qualified for any of it. He might have enough accounting knowledge and business savvy to keep Manelli Holdings on top with a good staff to prevent him from making any huge mistakes, but he'd never, ever considered becoming a father. Hell, he'd never wanted a serious relationship. He had friends. He had fun. And now he was the head of a company and somebody's dad. He didn't even have enough memories of Peter as a father to try to imitate him. The only parental words in his head belonged to their own father.

"In the Manelli house we don't call boys beautiful."

Audra's mom rose. "Dominic's right. The senior Manelli would have your head if he heard you call any Manelli male beautiful."

As Mary rounded her desk, Dominic watched the baby in her arms, unwittingly

37

realizing both Greene women were correct. Though his dad might have anyone's hide for calling a Manelli male beautiful, with his eyes closed in sleep and his round cheeks flushed pink Joshua was beautiful.

Audra laughed lightly. "He's stealing your heart, isn't he?"

And looking into her sparkling blue eyes, Dominic felt another tug of emotion. Except this tug had nothing to do with family love. This one was all about attraction. Audra's face glowed with life and vitality. Her full lips bowed into a smile so warm he felt it reach out and touch him. In one quick glance he saw and responded to the way her breasts strained against the pretty blue top she wore over a navy-blue skirt that subtly outlined a very shapely bottom.

Two weeks ago he'd have turned on enough charm to light New York City in a blizzard. Today he turned away. "I don't have time for anybody to be stealing my heart."

"And that scares you?"

It didn't scare him as much as it filled him with remorse, regret and even guilt. While Peter had gone looking for a wife, Dominic had had his pleasure with every woman who suited his fancy. While Dominic took trips to Monaco, Peter had studied. While Peter attended business meetings and summits with their father, Dominic hadn't paid more than a passing glance of attention at the family business.

Dominic had thoroughly enjoyed the past fifteen years that Peter had spent working, settling in, doing the right thing by the family. And now Dominic, the family playboy, suddenly had everything his brother had wanted — the business and the baby. He couldn't fail. He *refused* to fail, to let everything Peter had started fall to ruin. Yet Dominic didn't feel right taking charge, either. He was confused, grief stricken and in over his head.

All he really wanted was his own life back. The one he knew how to live.

Mary quietly said, "Do we now have someplace I can lay him down to sleep?"

Audra turned to the door. "The baby carrier is in the kitchen. I'll get it."

Dominic followed her. "I might as well bring the rest of his things to the nanny suite."

"Good idea."

"Then I'll accompany you to Olivia's, but after that I'm off to work."

Audra said, "That's fine. I can handle the furniture shopping this morning."

"Then this afternoon you can move in."

That comment stopped Audra dead in her tracks. For all her talk of getting up for 2:00 a.m. feedings, it hadn't sunk in that she'd have to move into the nursery while Dominic scouted a permanent nanny. Still, what difference did it make? She needed money. She was offering to be a nanny to get that money. And nannies usually lived in. No big deal. Especially considering Dominic was the epitome of the type of man she had sworn off forever.

She turned to tell him that she'd be moved in by the time he returned from work, but their gazes caught and she didn't see the fun teenager who had turned into a playboy. She saw a man who had lost his brother three months ago in a tragic accident and who had gained custody of Peter's son because of another family tragedy. Circumstances had made him serious and sad in a way that caused Audra's heart to awaken from a near year-long sleep. She felt it yawn and stretch and open again, as if welcoming him.

Any teasing comment she could have made froze on her lips. She might have been immune to the playboy, but would she really be safe with this guy? With a child to raise, he didn't have time to gallivant around the globe. He'd be underfoot. A brooding, sexy man aching for love. Like Heathcliff. What woman could resist that?

Worse, they would be living together. Running into each other in various stages of undress as they went about their morning and evening routines.

Still, it was too late to back out now. This deal was all about promises. She'd not only promised Dominic her assistance, but the Belles had promised Julie a wedding. And only she could earn enough money fast enough to pay for that wedding. One way or another she would resist him.

"Not a problem. I'll call the office and tell them I'll be out the entire day and move in this afternoon."

CHAPTER THREE

The trip to Marsha's mom's went smoothly. Audra did most of the talking, seeking information about Joshua's routine as they collected the rest of the baby's things and stuffed them into her little car. When everything was packed, she and Dominic went their separate ways.

As Dominic expected, the participants for his first meeting were already milling around his secretary's workstation when he arrived. He ushered them into his office, grabbing the pertinent files from his desk as they settled at the round conference table in the corner of the glass-walled room. That meeting bled into the next and the next and the next until his office suddenly emptied at six o'clock and he was alone.

Exhausted, he leaned back in his chair and pinched the bridge of his nose. This wasn't the end of his day. It should be. But at the point in time when he wanted nothing more than a glass of Scotch and some peace and quiet, he had a baby waiting for him.

Of course, Joshua now had a nanny of sorts. So the baby wasn't really *waiting* for him. He had company and was probably being entertained. Audra clearly knew what to do with the little guy. Which was more than Dominic could say for himself. He didn't know the first thing about changing a diaper. Forget about the more sophisticated end of the deal, like communication. He wasn't one to engage in baby talk. And the baby couldn't yet speak at all.

Plus he was tired. But edgy. Too restless to relax. The very last thing he wanted to do was inflict himself and his mood on a baby.

The blare of music from his cell phone into his silent office caused him to jump. He snatched it from his desk, peeked at the caller ID and groaned. As if it wasn't bad enough he'd had to give up his old life, certain friends from that life hadn't yet gotten the message that he could no longer come out to play. He nearly ignored the call, but in the end couldn't do that. He knew why Owen Bradley was calling. The man had scheduled the premiere of his movie in Boston specifically so Dominic could attend. If nothing else, Dominic had to apologize.

By eight o'clock that evening, Audra had finally stowed her belongings, including her laptop and a few client income tax files she needed to work on, in the suite Dominic had shown her. Settling into the rooms at the end of a long hall that led only to her suite, she realized most of her worries from the morning before had been unfounded. She and Dominic wouldn't be running into each other. She had no reason to be concerned an accidental meeting with gorgeous, brooding, Heathclifflike Dominic would turn into something neither one of them wanted. There would be no accidental meeting. She'd swear their quarters were so far apart they were in different zip codes.

Wearing a pair of jeans and a pink top from the extra clothing she'd brought, she tiptoed into the nursery just as Joshua awakened.

"Hello, sweetie," she said, pulling the baby from the crib, which had been delivered that afternoon and assembled by the estate handyman. Dressed in one-piece blue pajamas, Joshua blinked and yawned, stretching his little legs to their limits. But when his eyes focused and he looked at her, he began to wail.

"I know this is really hard on you." She kissed both of his cheeks. "You're not accustomed to me yet, so you're scared. But that's okay. You'll get to know me and you'll see there's nothing to be afraid of."

She continued cuddling and soothing him as she strode through the sitting room, down the winding staircase and the hall. Heading for the huge kitchen of the mansion, she said, "Let's go see my mom." She rubbed noses with the baby. "Remember her? She rocked you this morning."

The baby's crying slowed to sniffles, and he blinked at her. Using her hip she bumped open the swinging door and was surprised to find the kitchen dark. She fumbled for the light switch and flicked it on. The stainless-steel appliances and empty beige-and-gold-flecked countertops of the three islands greeted her.

Having watched her mother supervise the food preparations for many a party and too many formal dinners to keep count from this kitchen, Audra was accustomed to seeing the room full of life, energy and busy hands on Friday nights.

"Wow. Wonder where she is?" Her voice echoed hollowly around her in the huge, empty space. "She should be supervising service of some course or another of dinner right now."

"I'm not eating here tonight."

Audra swung around to find Dominic standing in the open doorway. Backlit by the lamps of the corridor behind him, he looked like a vision in his black tux, with his hair casually, sexily spiked and his hands tucked into his trouser pockets. Her breath stuttered just at the sight of him.

"I made arrangements to go out with friends."

"Oh." That was the only sound that would come out of her mouth. He was — quite literally — breathtakingly handsome.

"I thought I'd let you know I was going so you didn't come looking for me."

Her fogged brain finally picked up that he was leaving. As in going out. As in not going to be paying any attention to Joshua on his first night in the house.

So much for brooding Heathcliff.

"You're going?"

"Yes."

"But it's Joshua's first night here!"

"And if I hadn't hired you I couldn't have accepted the invitation."

Relief and understanding merged, and Audra's tense muscles relaxed. "Oh, it's business."

He flashed her a smile. "Monkey business."

His cocky attitude reminded her so much of her ex that any attraction she might have had to him flew out of the nearest window. She turned and walked back to the smallest of three stainless-steel refrigerators. The one she'd commandeered for all things Joshua.

"Dominic," she said his name using the scolding tone her mother had used with her when she wanted to go out on a school night. "You have a son now. You can't be going out just because the spirit moves you."

"First, Joshua is not my son. He's my nephew." He stepped into the kitchen, took an apple from a bowl on the first island and tossed it into the air, then caught it. "Second, having someone to stay home with the baby is why I hired you."

"No, you hired me to be a caretaker, not the love giver. Playing with Joshua, nurturing him, is your job."

He tossed the apple into the air again, ignoring her.

"I'm serious."

He didn't reply, and a horrible realization hit Audra. He didn't intend to nurture this little boy. Her heart caught with disbelief. Why would he refuse to be a dad to this adorable baby?

She glanced at blue-eyed, curly haired Joshua and decided Dominic simply hadn't spent enough time with him. Once he had, he wouldn't be able to help falling in love with him, and being a real dad would come naturally. And there was no time like the present to begin the process.

"Here." She handed Joshua to him. "Can you hold him while I warm a bottle?"

Having no choice, Dominic awkwardly took the confused baby. From the expression on his face as he fumbled to settle Joshua on his arm, Audra guessed that part of his sudden need to get out of the house might be his own fear.

"I can help show you how to care for him," she said, setting the bottle in the microwave and not looking at him, trying not to make a big deal out of it so he'd relax.

"I'm fine."

"Not really." She didn't think it prudent to mention that not being able to even hold the baby was a clear indicator that he wasn't fine. "I'm not talking about giving you actual baby lessons. But if you hang around us, especially while I'm here to help you bridge the gap, you could get to know Joshua by the time the permanent nanny gets here."

"I already know him." Struggling to contain the baby, whose confusion had become discomfort in his uncle-turned-father's arms, Dominic glanced over at her. "He's six months old. I've chucked his chin. I've said good-night to him when Marsha brought him into my brother's den before he went to bed. He was with us on boat trips and family stays at the beach house. The real problem between me and old Josh here," he said as he continued to wrestle the little boy, "is that I don't have a whole hell of a lot in common with a baby and he doesn't have the verbal skills to tell me about his day."

Audra couldn't help herself; she laughed. He was right. He and the baby didn't have a lot in common. Still, what baby and daddy did?

When the bell rang signifying the bottle was warm, she took it from the microwave and set it on the counter, then clapped her hands together and said, "Give him back."

Dominic was struggling with the baby, so Audra walked over to take the little boy. When she reached Dominic, simple, normal breathing brought the scent of freshly scrubbed adult male and spicy aftershave to her nostrils. Though tempted to inhale a long breath to catch the wonderful scent

49

completely, she resisted the urge, reminding herself that playboys were nothing but trouble.

But in the shuffle of clumsily handing a squirming six-month-old baby between them, fingers touched, arms brushed, and her chest tightened with the same tingle of anticipation she'd felt when she was twelve and she'd found him hiding in an obscure room somewhere in the family mansion. There was something about him that had called to her since she was old enough to realize the differences between boys and girls; and, whatever it was, it was powerful.

Still she ignored it. He wasn't the kind of guy she should be attracted to. Intent on getting them back to the conversation about Dominic spending time with Joshua to learn how to care for him, Audra pulled away with a smile. But when she caught Dominic's gaze and saw the smoky look in his eyes, she froze.

"Why don't you come out with me tonight?"

She swallowed. Oh, Lord.

"It's a premiere." He grimaced. "An action-adventure movie, but the star is a friend. I couldn't refuse." He stepped close, caught her free hand and caressed it. "We'll cut out early, grab dinner and maybe go dancing."

Audra pulled her hand from his. "Forget it, Prince Charming. I've had my fling with a playboy. I was engaged to a guy just like you. I won't be going that route again."

"You were engaged?"

"And he left me at the altar." She lifted the baby to Dominic's eye level. "But even if I didn't have that history, I have a better reason to stay here tonight."

Reminded of the baby, he winced. "Right."

"Just as you said, I'm here to help you with Joshua."

She said it crisply, evenly, sounding like a professional nanny. Or at least she thought she had, until Dominic leaned against the island, looking sexy, sophisticated and like a man who didn't believe a darned word she'd said.

"So, we'll postpone going out until I hire a permanent nanny."

She gaped at him. "I just told you I nearly married somebody like you and for my trouble got left at the altar. I eventually figured out that I pushed him into something he didn't want, but that only makes me know unequivocally that you're the last person I should go out with."

He chuckled, pushing away from the counter and stepping close. "Actually,

Audra, I think that makes me the perfect guy for you to go out with."

Though his nearness caused her pulse to skyrocket and her leg muscles to turn to rubber, her brain had jumped to full operating capacity. She gaped at him in disbelief, but before she could counter, he said, "Even you admit your mistake wasn't dating a playboy. It was thinking he would settle down."

She snorted a laugh. "Exactly."

"I think you missed your own point. You must have had good times with him." He caught her hand, lifted it to his lips. "Before you tried to tame him, that is."

She swallowed. A wispy trail of sensation danced along her knuckles, up her arm and flew straight to her heart. If a light kiss on her hand could make her insides shimmer with warmth, what would those lips do to her if they kissed her on the mouth?

"And didn't those good times make you happy? Maybe decrease your stress? Maybe help you forget your long week of work?"

"Yes." That was actually why she'd fallen in love with David. He was the first guy to make her forget everything. Let logic go. Leave her troubles on the dock as she stepped onto his boat. Laugh. Relax.

"And if you hadn't gotten serious with

him. If you'd let him be who he was . . . wouldn't you be together right now?"

And if *he* would let go of her hand, would her breathing restart? "No."

He laughed, pulling away from her. Not defeated, but looking like a guy who knew to retreat to fight another day. "I still say it wasn't him but your approach that was wrong. After I hire a new nanny, come out with me and have a little fun."

Audra sucked in a breath, amazed at how tempted she was to consider a suggestion that was incredibly wrong. He was too damned much like the man who had jilted her. And she'd learned her lesson. Dominic might be correct in saying that David had made her happy, but he'd skipped over the fact that she was a serious woman. She couldn't have uncomplicated relationships with men like her ex and Dominic. Anytime she got involved with a man she liked, she would always fall in love.

And that was the biggest reason of all to stay away from Dominic. She would fall head over heels and he would amuse himself for a few weeks or months and then move on.

No, thanks.

"Have fun tonight," she said, grabbing Joshua's bottle and heading for the door.

"And try not to stay out too late."

Joshua awakened four times that night. Obviously frightened and confused by another change of home and caregiver, the baby sobbed pitifully. Her heart breaking for the little boy who was experiencing his third change of homes in as many months, Audra rocked him, sang to him, cuddled and soothed him. It was 5:00 a.m. when they both fell into a deep sleep. So when Joshua's crying awakened her again, she groaned.

Sympathetic with the baby, she forced her eyes open only to discover it was morning. She popped up off her pillow, glancing at the clock. It was nine!

Throwing back the covers, she rolled out of bed and ran to the nursery. "Good morning," she sang, refusing to let herself be tired or listless when this baby so desperately needed love and understanding.

"We've got some stuff to do, and I'm not entirely sure what order to do it in." She kissed his forehead and then checked his diaper. Realizing he needed a change, she reached for one of the throw-away diapers in the drawer of the changing table beside the crib.

"For all my experience with my nieces,

I've never kept a baby overnight. When I babysat for my sisters, I always left when they returned home."

Done with his diaper, she lifted Joshua off the changing table. He blinked at her as she carried him out into the hall.

"Which means I've never handled a morning routine. Here's where we are right now. You need a bottle and probably a bath, but I also need to shower."

Having slept in a loose T-shirt and ankle-length pajama bottoms, she didn't feel uncomfortable walking through the house to the kitchen. "Since we both need things, I'm going to use what I call the airplane theory. The stewardess always says if a plane's in trouble and the oxygen masks drop, put on your own mask first, then you can help your child."

Joshua tilted his head as if trying to understand, but also as if growing accustomed to her. Her heart ached for him. He desperately needed someone, but it was wrong for him to be attaching to her. In a few weeks she'd be gone. She hoped Dominic wouldn't take forever to grow accustomed to him and get involved with him.

She kissed the baby. "That means I shower first, but I can't desert you while I shower, so we're going to enlist some help."

She bumped the swinging door open with her hip. Joyce Irwin, the weekend cook, sat on a stool at the center island. "Good morning, Joyce."

The short, thin brunette slid from her seat. She clapped her hands together with glee and her green eyes sparkled. "Oh! You have the little one!"

Audra winced. "Yes, but I need some help."

Joyce glanced at Audra's sleep-disheveled hair, rumpled T-shirt and pajama bottoms and nodded. "Your mom filled me in that we were to pitch in and do anything you asked. Do you want me to feed him while you shower?"

"Could you? He'll be occupied eating so he won't cry."

Joyce reached for Joshua. "Sounds like a plan."

"I'll be back in fifteen minutes. Twenty tops."

"Take your time. I raised a boy and a girl and have two grandkids. I'm a pro."

Audra said, "Thanks." But passing Joshua to the cook, she had a sudden vision of Joshua being raised by servants, getting his good-night kiss from whoever was in charge of putting him to bed that night, and it filled her with unbelievable sadness.

Telling herself not to think like that, she raced out of the kitchen and up the first two halls, but as she turned the corner for the third, she plowed into Dominic.

"Whoa!" he caught her by the shoulders and steadied her before setting her away from himself, his hands still loosely holding her.

Even on a Saturday morning, Dominic's first trip downstairs was made fully dressed in iron-creased trousers and an oxford cloth shirt — while she stood before him in pajama bottoms and a T-shirt, suddenly feeling like Cinderella. She might not be sweeping ashes for a wicked stepmother, but living with Dominic she would constantly be reminded of their different stations in life. Worse, the warmth of his hands on her shoulders seeped through her thin T-shirt and to her skin, sending a rush of heat through her entire body and causing her breathing to stop.

"Where are you going in such a hurry?"

She took one long breath to jump-start her lungs and, as calmly as she could, she stepped out of his hold. "Joshua and I had a long night. We just got up. I left him with Mrs. Irwin. So I could shower and dress." The accountant in her, the part that was always pulled together and capable, couldn't resist explaining why she looked so out of sorts. "That's why I'm —" She motioned to her big T-shirt and worn pajama bottoms with her hand. "Still in my nightclothes."

"Okay." In one word he managed to convey that he was both confused and amused by her explanation.

She wanted to shake herself silly. She didn't need to explain herself to him. She was a CPA. A professional. She wasn't Cinderella, tongue-tied with the prince.

And he wasn't Prince Charming. The prince she remembered from her storybooks would have picked up on the fact that she and Joshua had had a difficult night. He would have been concerned. *Dominic* should be concerned.

She stepped into his space again, angry that he'd missed the obvious. "The baby had a little trouble adjusting."

The light in Dominic's eyes softened. "I don't doubt it. Poor kid."

Okay. Sympathy. That was good. He wasn't totally indifferent. He had probably just missed her first mention of the baby having a long night. Or maybe he hadn't understood it. "Anyway, now that you're here, you can relieve Joyce."

His eyebrows knitted together in confusion. "Relieve Joyce?"

"Take Joshua from her."

"Can't. I have an informal business meeting at the club."

"But —"

"But nothing. I thought we went over this last night. This is why I hired you."

A voice inside her head told her to back off. She'd had a rough night and very little sleep, and he obviously had plans. Plans that were probably made long before he got the baby. Plus, pushing him into spending time with Joshua wasn't really her business.

The opposing voice told her it might not be her business, but Joshua was his child now and she couldn't bear to think of the baby living life without love, being kissed by servants, ignored by his family.

She listened to the second voice.

"Yes, we did go over this last night, and I thought you understood that you're Joshua's primary love giver."

To her complete amazement, he looked at his watch as if what she'd said was of little consequence. "Can we finish this later?"

She drew in a disbelieving breath. "No! Dominic, at some point —"

He brushed past her. "I'm late. We'll talk when I get home."

■ ■ ■ ■

Stepping into the backseat of his car, Dominic wished he hadn't called for his driver. Audra had made him so angry that he desperately wanted to slam a door. Now he couldn't.

Didn't she realize how hard this was for him? Didn't she see how much responsibility and work had already been thrust upon him? Didn't she understand he had so much to do that he was barely treading water? Didn't she own a real pair of pajamas?

The car door clicked shut behind him. His driver slid behind the steering wheel and Dominic burst out laughing. She was annoying, persistent, ill-informed — and so adorable he had wanted to flirt with her until she couldn't resist him. But she was also right. No matter how busy he was, he had a child to raise.

He had to get involved in Joshua's life, but as soon as he thought of spending time with him, he froze. He had absolutely no idea what to do with a baby. Worse, Peter was the strong, smart one. The one who should serve as Joshua's example. It didn't seem fair that Peter's little boy was stuck with second best. The guy who wasn't even sure how to hold him properly was the one who would teach him about life.

But Dominic knew the world wasn't always fair. Like it or not, he had to be more than a dad in name only. Maybe instead of teasing Audra, flirting with her or fighting, what he should be doing is taking advantage of her expertise while she was with him and Joshua.

CHAPTER FOUR

As Joshua woke from his nap that afternoon, the nursery door opened and Dominic walked in. Still furious with him, Audra wanted to lambaste him, but before she could open her mouth to speak, he handed her a bouquet of flowers.

"I'm sorry."

She tried to say, "That's okay," because an apology always warranted a second chance in Mary Greene's family. But looking at the bouquet of roses and daisies, an unlikely combination that for some damned reason or another made her happy, she was suddenly speechless. She hadn't been given flowers in a year. Not since her fiancé. She had literally forgotten how much fun it was to have someone think of her.

Joshua's crying jolted her back to reality.

"Oh, honey! I'm sorry!" She'd been so surprised by the flowers she'd forgotten the baby.

Dominic took a breath and hesitantly faced the crib. "I'll get him."

Audra's mouth fell open as Dominic leaned down to lift Joshua. "Hey, now. What's all this crying about?" He settled the baby's bottom on his forearm and grimaced. "My sleeve is now saturated."

"He had a long nap. His diaper is probably soaked."

"No 'probably' about it."

Audra reached for the baby but stopped herself. If their disagreement had led him to a change of heart, if he was really going to be the kind of dad this little boy needed, then he could start now.

"The diapers are in the top drawer of the changing table."

Panic flared in his eyes. "You're not going to change him?"

"Diaper changing is good bonding time."

"You've got to be kidding."

"My sister sang to her kids when she changed their diapers. When I babysat I realized singing's a good way to get everybody's mind off the messy business and onto something fun."

"I'm not singing to a baby."

"It'll be fun." She set the flowers on a handy table. "After I get a vase I'll teach you some cute songs —"

"Let me rephrase that. I'm not singing in front of anybody. Not even Joshua. I have a wickedly awful voice."

"No, singing career for you, huh?"

"Unless you want dogs in three states to howl."

She laughed. "The pitch that can only be heard by dog ears. You must be bad."

He handed Joshua to her and wouldn't meet her eyes as he said, "And I don't know how to change a diaper."

She figured as much. But she wouldn't make a big deal out of it. "That's okay. I'll teach you."

Rather than her offer reassuring Dominic, it seemed to panic him further. "How about if I go to my room, put on a clean shirt, send a maid with a vase, and come back for playtime?"

She wanted him to stay, but even she could see that changing a diaper the very first time he came into the nursery had overwhelmed him. Still, he'd said he would come back. This time yesterday, the wet shirt would have been an excuse for him to leave for good. Having him say he would return was progress.

"Okay."

Dominic left the room, and Audra kissed the baby's nose. "You're going to have playtime with your new daddy."

She laid the baby on the changing table, quickly realized He was a little worse off than she'd first imagined and headed for the bathroom. Holding the naked baby with one arm, she put the baby tub in the bathtub and started the warm water for him. Within seconds Joshua was up to his tummy in soap suds, happily slapping the water.

"Audra?"

"In here."

Dominic appeared at the door, wearing jeans and a T-shirt, his short dark hair disheveled just enough to be sexy, his dark eyes sparkling with their ever-present glimmer of mischief.

Tingles of warmth exploded in her stomach just from looking at him. He was cute. He was sexy. And now it appeared that he was owning up to his responsibilities with the baby. A natural urge to flirt with him bubbled up in her, but she squelched it. His willingness to spend a little time with the baby didn't translate to change in every area of his life. She couldn't get involved with Dominic. Flirting was out of the question.

Plus, he wasn't here for her. He was in the nursery to be with the baby. The most important thing in his life should be this little boy.

"He's already had a minute to play, so I'll just wash him up and bring him to the nursery."

Dominic said, "Okay," and stepped back, out of the bathroom.

Audra quickly washed Joshua, rolled him in a soft terry cloth baby towel and carried him into the nursery. "Would you like to dress him?"

"You're doing fine without me."

Once again she decided his refusal had more to do with inexperience than lack of desire, but she also realized that if he didn't stop making excuses, he might never grow accustomed to holding and caring for this child. And he had to. Joshua had been bounced from home to home since his parents' deaths. Now he was in his permanent home, but yet another primary caregiver, Audra, would be leaving. Dominic had to get involved with Joshua so the baby would have one stable, consistent, committed person in his life.

She turned away and made her voice as casual as possible as she said, "Okay. I'll dress him. Then you read to him."

"Great."

She faced him again, confused by his quick acquiescence. She'd expected to have to persuade him. Instead, he'd easily agreed.

The corners of his mouth tipped up sexily. His eyes sparkled. But there was something different about this smile than the ones he'd given her Friday night. Today he wasn't flirting. He was simply being himself. The Dominic her mother had always described. Fun. Friendly. Flirty. But not flirting. If stepping away from the baby when he was uncomfortable was his way of saying he wouldn't even try doing what he didn't know how to do, then his smile right now said he would do the things he was comfortable doing.

Accepting that, Audra dressed Joshua in a soft, one-piece romper with a train appliqué on the front, as Dominic browsed through the box of books they'd retrieved from Marsha's mom. When the last snap was snapped, she gave Joshua a teething ring before she handed him to Dominic.

Baby on his arm, he sat on the rocker. "All right, Joshua, we're going to read about a little train engine that goes up a mountain," he said, glancing through the pages.

Audra stifled a sigh of relief. Everything was going to be okay.

She hoped.

Turning away, she frowned. She wasn't one to put much stock in a wishy-washy emotion like hope. She was more of a planner. And the logical, organized accountant in her decided that since she couldn't force him to learn what to do with the baby, her only choice was to make sure Dominic spent enough time in Johsua's company that when her month of nannying was up, Dominic would at least be accustomed to the baby he now had to raise.

When Audra brought Joshua to the dinner table on Saturday night, Dominic frowned. "Isn't he a little young for filet mignon?"

She laughed, trying not to gawk around the gorgeous formal dining room, which was about the size of Audra's entire apartment. The high ceiling with three chandeliers placed equidistant above the gleaming mahogany table quietly spoke of the Manelli wealth. A long black, yellow and beige Oriental rug protected the marble floor. Pale-yellow walls accented the wainscoting. The yellow in the China pattern laid out on the table matched the walls.

Dominic stood at the head of the long table, where two dinner places had been set, and Audra noticed something she'd never seen before. Dominic was incredibly alone. Dressed in a dark suit with a white shirt and tie, he looked like a lonely prince, aching for love that he couldn't find.

Luckily she had enough sense to remind herself that he wasn't alone. Not only did he have myriad friends, but he also had a baby to raise.

"I didn't bring him for the filet mignon. I brought him for family time."

"You and I aren't family."

"No, but you and Joshua are." She glanced around. Not seeing the high chair she'd bought on Friday afternoon, she walked over to Dominic. "Take him a second while I go scout out the high chair."

Without thinking, she casually handed the wriggling baby to Dominic, and Dominic almost dropped him.

Realizing he hadn't been ready to take him, Audra said, "Sorry."

He said, "That's okay," but his mouth tightened in annoyance.

He was either seriously angry that she'd brought the baby to dinner or that she'd handed Joshua to him when he was unprepared to take him. Audra couldn't tell. Deciding that his irritation would pass — though she didn't want to leave him alone any longer than was necessary — she scrambled to the kitchen.

She found the high chair, carried it to the dining room, put it by his chair and said, "Set him in it," as she walked to the place set for her, to the right of Dominic.

He stood motionless for a few seconds. Then he smiled. He stepped in close and whispered in her ear, "Why don't you do it?"

She had no idea why he'd felt he had to whisper that, and with his warm breath tickling her ear, she couldn't muster the brain power to try to figure it out. Chills covered her body. Instinctively, she almost took Joshua, glad for a reason to step away from Dominic.

But sanity returned. Remembering he was the kind of guy who flirted with everyone, that there was nothing special happening between them and she had to stop acting like a ninny, she said, "Come on. Just set him in."

Dominic hesitated a second, but eventually turned to the high chair and slid Joshua behind the tray, trying to set him on the seat. Because she'd forgotten to open the tray, there was barely enough space to squeeze the baby through. Before she could rush over to open it, Joshua squirmed, angling one foot against the tray, and then used it as leverage to lunge forward, almost out of Dominic's arms.

"Damn it."

Audra leaped to the high chair and took

70

Joshua. "I'm sorry. I sometimes forget that you don't know how to handle a baby and you're not accustomed to the baby equipment."

"And I think you enjoy making me squirm."

His words were laced with such venom that Audra gasped. "I don't!"

He ran his hand along the back of his neck. His expression clearly conveyed that he couldn't believe he'd actually said that. "I know. I'm sorry." He took a breath. "Look, maybe I just need a break tonight." He headed for the door. "A few friends are meeting at a club. I'll see you in the morning."

"Wait!"

Too late. He was already through the swinging door.

She glanced at Joshua with a sigh. "I botched that big-time."

The baby laughed.

"Right. You won't thank me if your new daddy doesn't adjust to his role with you before a permanent nanny gets here and he has all the freedom in the world to stay away from you."

Dominic went to a noisy nightclub. He found a table full of his friends, ordered a round of drinks, grabbed a partner and began to dance.

And proceeded to have the worst time of his life. As if his world wasn't complicated enough, he felt guilty about his mini melt-down with Audra. He'd accused her of try-ing to make him squirm, not because he actually believed she'd done it deliberately, but as a knee-jerk reaction.

He'd spent his life being humiliated by a father who had constantly compared him to his older, smarter brother. On kind days, he and Peter would excuse their dad repeat-edly pointing out Dominic's deficiencies. It was his way of showing everyone why Peter would take the reins of the family business rather than Dominic. On normal days they both knew their father was a mean-spirited jerk.

Dominic tried to lose himself in the noise and the pulsing beat of the music and bod-ies in motion, but he couldn't. After a few hours of pretending to have fun, he sum-moned his driver and on the ride home came to the conclusion that he was as upset about not being capable with Joshua as he was about his meltdown.

He wasn't an idiot. And holding a kid, manipulating him into a damn high chair, shouldn't be so hard! It couldn't be. Ninety percent of the people in the world mastered it as parents.

Surely he could handle one measly baby!

On Sunday morning Dominic arrived in the nursery exactly as Audra had finished bathing Joshua and was walking out of the bathroom. This time, instead of flowers, he had coffee.

"The blue cup is yours." He set her cup on the dresser near where she would be working.

Audra glanced at her coffee and returned her gaze to his. He had been so frustrated the night before, she was sure he wouldn't even come in to say good morning. Yet he was back. And he looked about as cute as a man could look in his jeans and T-shirt, holding the mug of coffee he'd brought for himself.

"I'm sorry about last night."

"That was actually my fault. I should have opened the tray. I'm sorry."

He smiled hopefully. "So what we're really saying here is that we're both at fault. You should have remembered I'm not experienced, and I shouldn't have gotten frustrated over something I didn't know."

"Exactly."

He pulled in a breath and then pushed it

out noisily. "So what are we going to do this morning?"

Wrapped in his baby towel, chewing a blue teething ring, Joshua leaned toward Dominic.

"He wants you to take him."

Dominic placed his hands around the baby's ribs and took him into his arms. Joshua cooed up at Dominic, then as naturally as could be set his head on his uncle's shoulder.

Audra's heart melted. "Look how he likes you!"

A ripple of unease passed over Dominic's features before he swallowed hard. "Yeah. But I'll feel a lot more comfortable when his bottom is covered." He laid the baby on the changing table. "What do I do?"

"First, get a diaper."

Happy he was stepping up and asking questions, Audra reached for her coffee. Dominic leaned over to get a diaper from the dresser. Their arms brushed and, nervous, Audra jumped back.

Dominic grinned at her. "Sorry. We don't want you to spill your first coffee of the day." At her confused frown, he added, "Joyce told me you refused a cup this morning. She said you seemed to have your hands full with Joshua."

It gave her a funny feeling in the pit of her stomach that he had asked Joyce about her, but the jumpiness got worse when he glanced significantly at her worn T-shirt and scruffy pajama bottoms. She could have been embarrassed about her sleep attire, but it wouldn't matter if she were fully dressed. Everything about him gave her a jumpy feeling in the pit of her stomach. Even though she knew he was absolutely wrong for her, she couldn't seem to help being attracted to him.

Dominic held up the diaper, as if trying to make sense of it, turning it over in his hands, examining the size and shape. Recognizing that he didn't get the concept of the disposable diaper, Audra set the mug on the dresser again. She took the diaper from him and stepped closer to the table, which put her inordinately close to Dominic.

She'd thought there was room enough for her to step in, but suddenly she and Dominic were elbow to elbow. She could smell his clean scent, almost feel the heat radiating from him.

Telling herself she was simply hypersensitive to him because she'd had a crush on him for so long, she said, "It's like this." She displayed the diaper's two sticky tabs. "These two tabs go at the back." Holding

Joshua's ankles in one hand, she slid the diaper beneath his bottom with the other. "You slide the diaper under him like this, and then pull the front part up to cover him. Then open the sticky tabs on the side and pinch, pinch —" She pressed the tabs into place on the front. "And *voilà,* you're done."

Dominic leaned in, as if examining the diaper, but his upper arm brushed against her as he did. Her breathing shimmied in her chest. All her muscles tightened. She desperately wanted to shiver, but fought it.

"Looks simple enough."

He pulled back, his arm sliding against her again, setting off the same chain re-action he'd ignited when he'd leaned in. Except this time she couldn't stop the shiver.

He smiled at her. "Cold?"

"No." Because her voice came out like a breathless whisper, she cleared her throat. "No."

Reaching for the T-shirt she'd laid out for Joshua, Dominic jutted his chin in her direc-tion. "Do you own pajamas?"

All right. Now she could officially be embarrassed about her sleepwear. "No."

"You look like you belong in a college dorm."

She laughed. "Probably, since these things

are left-overs from my dorm days."

A few seconds went by in silence. Glad the topic of her sleepwear had died, Audra took a sip of coffee as she watched Dominic carefully pull the T-shirt over Joshua's head. He might not have done this before, but he obviously understood he had to be gentle with small bones and soft arms.

"I see you as a pink lace kind of girl."

She nearly spit out her coffee. "What?"

"Pink lace. You're not the red or black satin pajama type. You're more pink."

She gaped at him.

"Oh, okay. Maybe lace is too scratchy?" He looked back at her with a grin. "How about pink satin?"

He seemed so darned interested in her potential taste in pajamas that Audra's heart hammered. He could simply be talking about the first thing that came to his mind to give them a distraction while they performed simple tasks with the baby. But when he'd said pink lace, she'd seen a sexy little teddy and she'd bet her last dollar he had too. She sucked in a breath. She knew he was teasing, but what if he wasn't? Seriously. What would she do if he was genuinely interested in her?

The answer came quickly. Easily. She would do nothing. Getting left at the altar once by a guy just like him was plenty. She didn't want to go through that a second time. Plus, he should be focused on the baby, not her.

"Since Joshua's our top priority, I can't think of a reason in the world why we'd need to be discussing my sleepwear."

He laughed. "Come on, Audra. I'm just trying to lighten the mood."

Feeling like a shrew she said, "All right."

He peeked askance at her. "But you have to admit we do have a bit of chemistry."

"Unfortunately."

"Oh, that's right. I forgot that you lump me in with your ex."

Not about to argue that, Audra said nothing. Dominic finished dressing Joshua, lifted him from the table and handed him to Audra.

"But I still think you're missing out." He touched the tip of his finger to her nose and then headed for the door. "I have a few things to do today. I might not be back."

Audra stared at the door. Her lungs had frozen. Her head was spinning. He could reduce her to a puddle just talking about the fact that they had chemistry.

And once again he was gone.

CHAPTER FIVE

On Monday morning Audra left Joshua in the capable hands of her mother and the staff, drove down the tree-lined lane of the Manelli estate and headed for the bank. Her functional black leather purse contained a check for fifty thousand dollars paper-clipped to a deposit ticket — the first half of the money to save Julie's wedding.

Or not.

Right now she wasn't sure what she should do.

She hadn't seen Dominic since he'd left her and Joshua on Sunday morning. She knew he had been around the house, mostly in his office, but he'd never returned to the nursery, not even to check up on Joshua. On Sunday night she'd heard through the staff grapevine that he'd gone out with friends.

Because he trusted her . . . so much that he didn't feel the need to peek in on Joshua to see if he was okay, and that wasn't good for Joshua. If she put this check in the bank and stayed on as Joshua's nanny, she ran the risk that Dominic wouldn't spend enough time with the baby. On the other hand, every time he came into the nursery, he reduced her to a quivering mass of attraction.

In theory, squelching the attraction should be a simple matter of remembering the fiancé who'd left her at the altar. But David was the last person who popped into her head when a simple brush of her hand against Dominic's had her heart thrumming. All she could think about Sunday afternoon was what if he kissed her one of these days? Could she pull back? Tell him to behave? Or would she melt?

The intelligent part of Audra Greene recognized that adding sexual chemistry to her simple schoolgirl crush had created some sort of firestorm that was sucking her in like a black hole. That part of her knew the smart thing to do would be to get away from him. That meant either give back the check and get out of his life, or keep the check but keep her distance.

But if she kept her distance, would she be keeping Joshua away from the man who was supposed to be his daddy?

On a groan of frustration, she drove to the Wedding Belles offices and entered the townhouse with the check squished in her coat pocket. Part of her genuinely believed she needed to give Dominic back his money and get the heck away from him. Another part equally believed she was strong enough to resist a little flirting. She might still have a few weeks left with him, but she could be very strong when she needed to be. Why was she so afraid?

"Good morning, Audra!" At her desk in the foyer, which served as a reception area for the business, radiant, happy Julie beamed at Audra.

Audra pasted on a smile. "Good morning."

"Everybody's getting settled in the conference room for the emergency meeting you called on Friday."

Audra stopped dead in her tracks, turned and faced Julie again. "Meeting?"

"You sent out an e-mail on Friday morning, saying we needed to have an emergency meeting. Then you left for the day and when you called saying you wouldn't be back until this morning everybody assumed that meant you wanted to have the meeting first thing today."

She'd forgotten all about that e-mail. Now

she had the Belles sitting in the conference room, waiting for her.

"Sorry I can't join you," Julie added, pointing at the stack of envelopes on her desk. "Mail came early."

Audra nodded, feeling the hand of fate at her back. In her head, she might be able to tell herself she could resist Dominic, but her heart wasn't convinced. She was afraid. With Julie busy at the reception desk and the Belles gathered for a meeting, it was as if fate had created the perfect opportunity for Audra to admit they were out of money. Then Audra could call a temporary nanny service and make arrangements for someone to be at Dominic's house that night, give back his check and save herself from a situation that was beginning to feel all too familiar.

Squaring her shoulders, she headed down the hall. With one quick meeting she could settle this problem once and for all. Head high, she walked into the conference room.

"Hey," Callie Philips-Faulkner said. Blond with green eyes that sparkled with life, Callie was one of Audra's best friends. "It's about time you got here."

Audra set her briefcase on the table and reached for the buttons of her coat. "I was a bit delayed."

"Yeah, an hour," Natalie Thompson said with a laugh. A petite blonde with a smattering of freckles, Natalie was the fresh-faced innocent of the group. "You're never late for work."

Mug of coffee in hand, stylish Serena James slid in beside Audra. "That's so not like you! What's up?"

Audra took a breath. "Belle, would you mind closing the door?"

Belle rose from her seat at the conference table. Though Belle was the owner of Wedding Belles she was also a true Southern belle, with a warm heart and a generous personality. "Sure, sugar."

Audra took another breath, her gaze going from one smiling, expectant face to the next. But before she opened her mouth to tell them about their dwindling funds, something incredible struck her.

This time last year, she had been the one happily in love. Every one of the ladies in front of her had been alone. Today they were all married or engaged.

Floral designer Callie had married Harry Faulkner.

Photographer Regina and her husband Dell O'Ryan had patched up their difficulties.

Cake whiz Natalie had married Cooper

Sullivan.

Master dressmaker Serena had fabulous Kane.

General assistant Julie was engaged to the love of her life, Matt.

Even Belle had Charles Wiley.

And Audra — the one so smitten with David that she hadn't realized he'd been panicking and about to dump her — was alone.

Except she was smarter now. Having been dumped had changed her. Made her wary. Wasn't she wary of Dominic? Of course she was. She wasn't flirting with him. Didn't show any signs of actually melting in his presence. She *felt* things but didn't act on them. She *wouldn't* date another guy like her ex. She really had learned her lesson.

She stood a little taller. She could resist flirty Dominic.

"I called this meeting to tell you —"

And since she knew she could resist Dominic, it didn't make sense to snatch away the opportunity the Belles had to keep their promise to Julie.

"— that in spite of the Vandiver wedding cancellation, our pocketbook is still in great shape."

Belle laughed and patted her perfectly coiffed silver hair as she rose from her seat.

Standing in front of Audra, she pressed both of her palms to Audra's cheeks and then planted a kiss on her nose. "Only you, sugar, could scare us to death with an ominous e-mail calling a meeting to tell us we're doing fine."

Callie collapsed in her chair. "Sheesh, Audra, we've got to teach you some new communication skills."

Serena rose and headed for the door. "The next time you have good news, Audra, put a smiley in the reference line of your e-mail."

The other girls mumbled similar agreement, and within a few seconds the busy wedding planners had gone back to their respective jobs. Audra took a breath.

"Something troubling you, sugar?"

Audra glanced at Belle, who stood by the coffee carafe, holding a mug of the coffee that Julie always brewed for their meetings.

"No."

"I know you. You hold your cards close to the chest. You don't ever feel the need to apprise us of our finances. You consider it your job to handle anything that comes up with our money. You'd never call a meeting to give us good news. Because you did call a meeting, I'm guessing you have news so bad you didn't think it fair to keep it from us, but panicked at the last minute and couldn't tell us."

Audra swallowed, gathering her briefcase, purse and coat. "No. I simply realized on Friday morning that you all might be worried that the Vandiver wedding cancellation had hurt our finances." She smiled. "I really did just want to tell you all that we're fine."

"If we weren't fine, you would tell at least *me,* right?"

Audra slid her right hand behind her back and crossed her fingers. "Absolutely."

"You know I'm a tough old broad. I can pretty much handle anything."

Something stirred in Audra's chest. She'd spent her life keeping her troubles to herself, sharing a bit with her mom, but not everything. Not the depth of her humiliation at being left at the altar. Not the fear that surfaced after David's rejection that she'd always be alone. Not the stinging recrimination that she was so logical she was a nag. And she certainly couldn't tell her mother that her employer was flirting with her daughter.

But looking at Belle she suddenly longed to confide. Life had handed Belle plenty of troubles, and she'd weathered them well. She wasn't merely smart. She was wise because of all the things she'd been through.

Belle studied Audra's face. "There's

86

definitely something you're not telling me."

Audra coughed nervously, not accustomed to showing weakness. "It's nothing."

"Ah, sugar, let me help you." Belle took Audra's hand and patted it as she lowered herself to one of the plush chairs around the conference room table. "Come on. Sit."

Audra sat.

"So what's up?"

Though she desperately wanted to confide, she wasn't ready to share her humiliation about David. She wasn't even sure she could talk about Dominic. But she really needed some advice. So maybe the thing to do would be approach it backhandedly?

"I have a friend whose boss is a little flirty."

Belle's eyebrows rose in question, then she laughed lightly. "A little flirty?"

"Well, he's —" Because she was hiding her nanny job from the Belles, Audra could see no reason to deviate from that part of the story. "My friend is working as a nanny for a very wealthy, very handsome guy. He just got custody of his nephew and he has absolutely no baby skills."

"Oh, poor guy."

"When his brother died, my friend's new boss also had to take control of the family business and he's overwhelmed."

Belle shook her head. "Wow."

"So you think he's got a valid point when he says he's having trouble adding the baby into his life?"

"Oh, sugar, working and parenting are both hard. Blend them together and a person's private life is all but gone." Belle leaned her elbow on the conference table and placed her chin on her closed fist. "That's probably why he's flirty. He misses going out."

"Yes, I think that's part of it." Audra squirmed on her seat. "But my friend also tells me that she and her boss have a lot of chemistry."

"So why don't they date?"

"He's dropped a few hints in that direction, but they're not suited. He's rich. She's normal. Plus, he's not cut out to be a family man, so she knows he would never consider a permanent relationship with her."

"He'd never consider anything permanent but he wants to sleep with her?"

Audra thought that through. "I don't think it's quite like that."

"I still don't like it," Belle said without hesitation.

"But even you said it makes perfect sense."

"No, I didn't! I said it makes sense that he's overwhelmed by the baby."

"So that's why he's flirting —"

"Audra, you're twisting this to make a scoundrel seem like a good guy."

Audra gaped at Belle. "That's not fair. You don't even know him."

"I don't know the girl, either, but I can tell you some things about her. If she's tolerating a boss flirting with her, she's got very low self-esteem. Probably she's recently been hurt."

"She has, but her self-esteem is fine. She's definitely over her hurt and able to handle herself."

Shaking her head, Belle rose from her seat. "I hope so."

"She is."

Belle stopped at the door. "If she continues to work with that guy — whatever her reason — she needs to set him straight. If nothing else, flirting with an employee is out of line."

With that Belle left the conference room, closing the door behind her. Audra fell back on her seat. A headache formed at her temples. She might be strong enough to resist Dominic, but she'd forgotten one important detail. As her employer, Dominic was out of line. And Belle was right. She had to set him straight.

Shrugging into her coat again, she walked

through the reception area to the front door.

"Where are you going?" Julie called after her.

"Bank. I have a check I have to deposit."

"You're doing very well with him."

Dominic kept his attention on dressing the baby for bed, feeling odd. Not only was Audra behaving stiffly and formally, but also the baby had been inordinately happy to see him. The chubby cherub on the changing table grinned toothlessly at him, making spit bubbles in the corners of his mouth, gooing and cooing, as if joy spilled from him.

With the little boy warm and squirming under his hands — very real, very human, very vulnerable, yet somehow very sweet — the truth of his situation plowed into Dominic. *He* was Joshua's parent now. *He* was responsible for raising him. And the only parenting example he had was bad.

Grateful that Audra was helping him, he said, "If I'm doing well, it's because I have a good teacher."

She walked to the rocker and bent in front of the bookcase to choose a book. "Don't get too cocky. You're not a pro."

He *knew* something was bothering her. "I might not be a pro. But I'm good enough to handle him in an emergency."

Book in hand, she faced him. She took a breath that shifted her breasts beneath her simple yellow T-shirt, drawing Dominic's attention to them. He nearly said something flirty, if only to get her out of her bad mood, but suddenly realized she was right. He wasn't a pro, and the kid currently squirming against his palms was his now. *His.* He couldn't alienate the one person in his life who was helping him.

"I know you think you're too busy to spend time with Joshua, but also I think we could fix that with a good schedule."

All right. He might not want to alienate her, but sometimes her ideas were a bit extreme. "You want me to create a schedule to spend time with my own family?"

"Yes."

Dominic turned his attention to fastening the snaps of the outfit of a baby who cooed at him, touching his heart when he thought his heart was untouchable, once again making him feel Audra was correct. He should spend more time with Joshua.

But how? His schedule was already filled to capacity.

"Don't look at scheduling time with Joshua as a bad thing," she said. "When a parent works, schedules are sometimes necessary."

"I live and die by schedules, now that I've taken over the family business." And because he had the same pressures his father had, Dominic could actually surpass his father in inadequacy. "I know how important they are."

Audra nodded at the baby in his arms. "So be a little flexible, then. This baby has lost his parents. All he needs is a piece of your time."

He glanced at the baby again, his chest squeezing with panic. He'd always said having no time at all with his father would have been better than the miserable hours he'd spent in his presence. And maybe the same was true for Joshua?

"You know, Audra. This is kind of pointless. I'm hiring a nanny. She'll take care of Joshua." He handed Joshua to her and headed for the door.

"Yes, but —"

"No buts." He didn't hear the rest of her protest as he walked out of the nursery. He'd think long and hard about the potential damage he could inflict on Joshua before he'd be back.

If he came back at all.

Chapter Six

When Audra brought a clean and bathed Joshua into the kitchen on Wednesday morning, Joyce greeted her.

"Good morning, Audra."

"Joyce?"

"I'm working Wednesdays so your mom can care for the little one." She handed Audra a mug of coffee. "She said to tell you to bring him into her office. And then Dominic asked that you have breakfast with him."

Audra's heart stopped. He wanted to have breakfast with her? Oh, Lord. He was either going to apologize or fire her. And after the way he'd walked out the other day she was expecting to be fired.

Of course, Dominic had a way of surprising her. She hadn't thought he wanted any involvement with the baby at all, and he'd at least made an attempt with Joshua. It had been push and pull with him right from the beginning. If he held to his normal pattern,

Monday he pushed and today he'd pull. He would apologize and be back in the nursery that night.

She took the mug of coffee and rushed through the short hall in the back of the mansion to her mom's office. As she stepped into the room, her mom rose. "Good morning, sweet baby," she said, holding out her hands to take Joshua.

"Hi, Mom. Can't talk. Dominic has requested my presence at breakfast."

Mary grimaced. "He's been up since five, sitting in the dining room reading the paper." She glanced at her watch. "For two hours. You might want to get a hitch in your get-along."

Audra nodded and raced out of her mother's office. If he had gotten over what had panicked him, wanted to apologize and wanted to arrange a time to be with Joshua that night, she couldn't afford to miss this chance. Knowing it would take her at least twenty minutes to shower and dress, and considering the potential decline in Dominic's mood if she made him wait another twenty minutes, she decided to eat breakfast in her baggy pajama bottoms and oversize T-shirt, and ran through the kitchen, retracing the path from her mother's office.

She made it to the swinging door that connected the kitchen and dining room in what she considered to be record time. With a bump of her shoulder, she opened it, burst into the "every day" dining room and stopped dead in her tracks.

She'd never seen this room before, but had been told it was a simpler version of the formal dining room. Audra had expected something casual and homey. Instead the room screamed old money. The pale blue and delicate yellow tapestry cushions of the chairs corresponded with the blue-and-yellow pattern on the china and the yellow of the walls. An oval taupe-, beige- and sand-colored Oriental rug sat on the hard-wood floors below the table. She swallowed.

"Good morning."

Dressed in a black suit, white shirt and red print tie, Dominic sat at the head of the table, reading the paper, looking very much like a lord or prince or maybe even a king.

She swallowed again, suddenly understanding why The worn clothing she used as pajamas seemed so strange to him. Luxury wasn't something he indulged in every once in a while. Luxury was a way of life for him.

"Are you joining me for breakfast?"

Realizing she was standing staring at him and his surroundings like an idiot, she headed for the place that had been set, assuming it had been arranged for her.

"I was told you commanded my presence."

He chuckled. "Not hardly. I have a feeling no one commands you to do anything."

"You should talk!"

"Excuse me?"

Audra nearly groaned. Why did she keep pushing him? She took a breath as she sat at her place at the table. "I'm sorry, but you're a heck of a lot worse than I am when it comes to doing what you want when you want."

Sherry, one of the downstairs maids, appeared with a plate and set it in front of Audra.

"I hope you don't mind. I asked Joyce to prepare the same breakfast for you as I'm having. It simplifies things for her."

She glanced at the plate of eggs and bacon. A funny feeling settled in her chest. All right. So he was considerate with the staff? It still didn't help Joshua one iota.

But she'd done enough back talk already with that one slip. "No. I don't mind. This is great."

He folded the newspaper. "Unfortunately, because it took you so long to get here, I'm done eating and need to get moving."

Now she remembered why she constantly pushed him. He always pushed her first. "Can't put a stop watch on a baby or his time. I do what Joshua needs when he needs it."

To Audra's surprise he laughed. "No kidding." He reached to his left for a huge box. Wrapped in sunny yellow print paper and tied with a big white bow, it was large enough to contain a full-length fur coat.

Setting the box on the empty space between their place settings, he said, "Here. For you."

"I don't want —"

"Consider it a gift for me."

That got her curiosity up. "For you?"

"For me." He angled his head in the direction of the box. "Come on. Humor me."

She took a breath and rose. The box was so big she had to stand to reach the bow. Luckily, the lid had been wrapped separately and she only had to lift it to reveal the contents of the box.

When she saw the blue-and-white-striped shirt, she glanced at him. "What's this?"

His eyes danced with delight. "Pull it out."

She lifted the shirt and saw that beneath it lay matching plain blue pants. "Pajamas?"

"Ten pairs."

She pulled out a second pair. Pink boxers

and a tank top. A yellow nightshirt. A set of red long-sleeved man's cut. A multicolored floral nightgown that reached the floor. Navy blue polka dot. Green triangles on a white background. Plain blue. Sunny yellow.

And at the bottom were pink satin man's cut trousers and a long sleeved top.

Not a pink lace teddy amongst them.

She didn't know whether to be insulted or to laugh. In the end the laugh won, bubbling from her chest. She peered at him. "Are mine really that bad?"

"Yes, but I also felt odd about walking out on you the other night."

He caught her gaze. The look in his dark brown eyes sent a sizzle through her. "I panicked. Again." He drew a long breath. "I'm afraid about this whole dad thing. I want to be a good dad, but I'm not sure I can be."

"Of course you can —"

"Audra, not only did I have a terrible example in my dad, but also my time is stretched to the limit. I expected to have a few minutes for Joshua yesterday morning but got called to a meeting. That's how the rest of my life is going to be."

"You were intended to come into the nursery yesterday?"

"Yes. But I never found time."

She took a breath. "Then I'm going to apologize, too."

One of his dark eyebrows rose. "Really?"

She laughed. "I know I'm probably more forward than any nanny you'd hire for real. But that's because I'm not really a nanny. I'm a CPA, remember?"

He rolled his eyes. "I remember." Then he smiled. "Actually, I like that about you."

"That I'm a CPA or that I'm forward?"

"You might be forward, but you keep me on my toes." Laughing, he shook his head. "That's probably why I have to wrestle myself not to flirt with you. I don't want to lose you." He rose. "But I think we're making a mistake in ignoring this thing that's between us."

She set the pink satin pajamas back in the box, ready to put an end to this discussion once and for all by talking about the possibility of them dating for real. Not as a joke. Or as something they flirted about. But in the real world. In a real way. "You don't even know me."

He nodded at the box again. "Look at those and tell me I don't know you."

Her gaze fell to the pajamas. Pretty colors. Imaginative prints. Lots of fun. Yet still practical. And no inappropriate pink lace teddy.

She caught his gaze. "All right. So you do have a certain understanding."

He rose, laid his linen napkin on his plate and stepped away from his chair. "A certain understanding?" He laughed. "Honey, you and I are very much alike, except we come at it from different directions. I have no time because I have a ready-made career that demands every second I can spare and I long for a little bit of fun. You need every ounce of your time to make your place in the world and you long for somebody to whisk you away . . . even if it's only every once in a while." He caught her gaze again. "Whisking you away would give me just the right amount of my old life back and being whisked would give you just the right amount of your old life back."

He walked to her side of the table, where she stood beside the big box of pajamas, caught her hands and kissed her forehead. "But I respect your wishes."

The brush of his lips sent a rush of tingles to her toes. Her entire body went on red alert, waiting for his mouth to smooth down her temple and capture hers.

Instead he pulled back and walked away. Looping around the long cherry-wood table, he headed for the door at the opposite end of the room and without a backward glance left her alone in the dining room.

Her gaze fell to the pajamas. Acknowledgment rose inside her. He knew her. He saw the playful side most people didn't see. He understood her practical side. He wanted to whisk her away. But she didn't want to be whisked, and he respected her wishes.

He might be a player, but he was nothing like David.

The door from the kitchen opened and her mother strode in. "Dominic gone?"

Audra returned to her place at the table and lifted her fork. Though she had no appetite, if she didn't eat, her mother would ask why, and then she'd be forced to explain that she had made some terrible judgments about her boss.

"He said he'd waited long enough for me."

Mary glanced at the pajamas. "What's this?"

"Seems your boss doesn't like my sleepwear."

Mary laughed. "You do bear some resemblance to a ragamuffin."

Audra huffed out a breath. "I'm not exactly sure what difference it makes. These work."

"Yes, but they aren't fun." Audra's mom

picked up the navy-blue polka dot set and laughed. "These are cute."

"Yeah, a regular laugh riot."

"Come on. He's only trying to lighten things up a bit. And he may not even be doing it for you. He's been horribly down since his brother died. Maybe he did this more for himself. To give himself a laugh."

Audra nearly groaned. All this time she'd been worried about protecting herself from him, when he'd been struggling with grief over his brother. And she'd been critical, insensitive. She fought not to squeeze her eyes shut in misery.

"Honey, I'm not blind. In the past year, you've sunk into the doldrums. It's time to come back to the land of the living. Have some fun."

She took a breath, let it out slowly. Was she so sad-looking that even a man who was grieving felt sorry for her?

Great. That made her feel just peachy.

"Once Dominic has a nanny, I'll take a long, hard look at my life."

"Okay." Audra's mom reached into her dress pocket and pulled out an envelope. "I'm not just here to harass you," she said as she handed the envelope to Audra. "From Dominic."

Audra's voice dropped an octave. "Oh."

"I'm guessing this is your way to get the Wedding Belles out of trouble."

She caught her mother's gaze. "But he already gave me the check."

"He told me to tell you that he's giving you the second installment early."

Audra stared at the check. "He doesn't want me to back out."

"Why would you?"

"He hasn't exactly been there for Joshua. And I sort of push him. I have to remind him to even pop into the nursery to say hello. Forget about helping with bath time or bedtime. Once or twice he's come in, but as a general rule, he forgets."

"Because he's busy, but also that's what he knows. Dominic and Peter were both raised by nannies. It's what people with money frequently do. You shouldn't interfere. Especially not if it makes him feel even worse than he already does over the loss of his brother."

"I get it."

"Okay. So no more pushing. Go put your check in the bank, save the Belles and be happy."

Audra laughed. There was that word. *Happy.* She rose from the seat and walked around the table to kiss her cheek. "Thanks, Mom."

But she seriously wondered if she would ever be happy again. She seriously wondered if she was even meant to be.

CHAPTER SEVEN

In spite of the mother's suggestion that Audra needed to be kinder to Dominic, when he went out with his friends that night, she was so angry with him that she could have spit nails. How had this run-around fooled everybody into thinking he was a sad, lonely guy? Especially her astute mother? He might be grieving the loss of his brother. He might even be overwhelmed with work. But he always seemed to have time for fun. And as for needing to whisk her away? Huh! He seemed to be able to work entertainment into his life just fine without her. And his "whisk her away" line was exactly that. A line. A come-on.

She fell into a fitful sleep and awakened at two o'clock, thinking Joshua had cried for his middle-of-the-night feeding. When she walked to the crib, she found the baby sound asleep. Realizing her body was so at-tuned to the wake-up call that now she was getting up before Joshua cried, she waited a few minutes for him to stir. When he didn't, her heart swelled with hope. Maybe the baby was finally adjusting to the strange house, strange crib and strange people now caring for him.

She crawled back under the covers and closed her eyes, but sleep wouldn't come. Whipping back the blankets, she rolled out of bed and went to the kitchen for something to help her relax.

Familiar with the cabinets, she walked directly to the one housing the cocoa, pulled the syrup from the cupboard and went in search of a microwave-safe mug. Just as she hit the start button to heat the milk and chocolate she'd mixed, the kitchen door swung open and Dominic burst in, his chiseled face drawn in serious lines, looking like a guy about to confront an intruder.

"Oh, it's you."

He was so sexy in a tux that no matter how angry she was with him, the female in her simply couldn't stifle the flutter in her tummy. She allowed herself the small tingle of appreciation just looking at him gave her. Then she realized he'd heard her noise and investigated, and she laughed. "You thought a burglar got thirsty, didn't you?"

His confront-the-intruder tension now

gone, he strolled into the room. "I don't know what I thought. I heard a noise as I entered the foyer. I'm not accustomed to having someone in the house prowling around in the middle of the night."

"Because you haven't yet become accustomed to having a baby. If you'd spent more time with Joshua, you'd remember you hired a nanny and that said nanny *will* be prowling around at all hours."

He snorted a laugh. "Right. As if it's that simple to unlearn thirty-six years of behavior."

"You could if you tried," Audra insisted, though her mother's words about Dominic only living what he knew haunted her.

"I don't think so," he said equally confident. "I wasn't the one who prepared for this baby for nine months. I wasn't even supposed to be the one who raised him when his parents died. Marsha's mother was."

"Maybe you haven't been prepping for this, but you were learning. Yet you didn't even come into the nursery to say hello today."

The microwave buzzer sounded. Audra reached in for her cocoa. Slamming the door closed she added, "Even if you never change a diaper or dress him again. You still

107

need to come in and say hello in the morning and good night in the evening."

"When I'm home and not busy, yes, I will do that."

She shook her head. "This isn't a matter of doing things when convenient. This is important. My dad died when I was a little girl and I grew up understanding that my mom didn't have a lot of time for me, but she still made *some* time. And I'll bet your busy dad made some time for you, too. Maybe not entire days. Maybe not hours at a clip. But I'm sure he said hello and good-bye. Asked about your grades and baseball games. Checked in with you every day."

"He did, but any real time he had went to Peter. Peter was the one being groomed to take over the business." He caught her gaze. "And before you start overanalyzing that, I'll tell you that I accepted that, too. I respond very well to reason and logic."

"You just made my point. You're looking at your relationship as if Joshua is you in your dad's life. But he's not. He's Peter. Joshua's the one who's going to take over the family business. You have to treat him the way your dad treated Peter."

The expression on Dominic's face crumbled into one of confusion. "The kid is six months old."

"Doesn't matter. The bonding starts now."

He groaned.

Audra grinned triumphantly and issued the challenge. "If you really take your role seriously, you have to raise Joshua the way Peter was raised."

He stared at her, clearly confronted by something he couldn't explain away, not even to himself. After a few seconds he half laughed. "Even though my dad was fairly decent with Peter, he's not the kind of dad a smart guy copies."

"Then just do what comes naturally."

"Right." He shook his head. "What has always come naturally to me is schmoozing." He glanced around the kitchen, as if disoriented. "But I'm even losing that. I'm so focused on spreadsheets and expansion plans that I sometimes forget how to make simple conversation. I had a miserable time tonight. I can't even remember what fun feels like."

"The world is sort of turned upside down?"

He caught her gaze. "Yes."

She opened her arms and spread her hands. "Look who you're talking to. I can't remember what it feels like to be happy. You want to hear about a world turned upside down? I stood in the back of a church, sequins sparkling and bouquet in hand, ready to commit to someone who didn't even have the courtesy to call my cell and tell me he'd changed his mind. In one short hour I went from believing my life was perfect to being rejected and wondering how I'd get through the next day."

"I'm sorry."

Though others had sympathized, Audra had never believed anybody understood what had happened to her life, her heart, her soul . . . her *everything* until Dominic. One event had changed his entire life, too. They had both lost not just a love or a brother. They'd lost the future they'd envisioned awaited them — a future they knew how to deal with — and were forced into a life that some days didn't even make sense.

She took a breath. "Thank you for the sentiment, but you weren't at fault."

"Maybe I'm apologizing on behalf of rich bad boys everywhere who should know better than to trick some nice girl into thinking we'll settle down."

A delighted giggle burst from Audra. A year ago she might have agreed he should apologize, if only on principle. But time and distance really had given her perspective enough that he'd made her laugh.

He smiled. "See, that's the kind of stuff I

used to be good at. Making people laugh. Making them feel good. Now everybody wants me to be serious. Smart." He shook his head. "I think a few of the people on the board would like me better if I'd rant and rave."

"So save your sense of humor for Joshua. It's really very easy to make a baby laugh and like you. All you have to do is tickle his tummy. You can recite the Declaration of Independence while you're tickling. It doesn't matter what you say, he only wants to hear your voice."

Dominic rubbed his hand across the back of his neck. "Audra, even if I did believe you, I don't have time."

She started to speak, but he held up a hand to stop her.

"Before you remind me that I made time to go out, the biggest reason I'm not having fun is that I've been entertaining business associates — doing the job I used to do for Peter. I might not be the fun guy I used to be, but I still have to soften up the people I need to do business with so they're predisposed to trust me and do the deals I need done. What everybody seems to forget is that this — schmoozing — was my job for the company. When Peter died I was waiting in the wings to replace him. When I replaced him, no one stepped up to do my job."

"So maybe you need to hire a schmoozer?"

Dominic blinked. Rather than feel sorry for him, once again Audra had challenged him. He wanted to wallow. She kept nudging him to answers. But she didn't have every piece of the puzzle.

"You have a simplistic view of the world."

She shrugged. "I think you have a skewed view of the world. Not everything's black-and-white."

"Then it appears that we have to agree to disagree."

"I'll accept that, if you can answer one question for me."

"Anything to get to bed."

"What did Peter do with Joshua? How was he involved in his life?"

Dominic drew a quiet breath. "I didn't live with Peter so I don't know." But he did know. He saw Peter with Joshua every time the family got together. He'd heard stories from Marsha about Peter getting up for two-o'clock feedings and changing diapers.

"Make an educated guess."

"Okay," he said, getting angry now. "What if he was doing exactly as you said, bonding over simple daily things like feedings and diapers? He might have had a business to run and a family to squeeze in, but he had a wife to help him and he had me." Fury unexpectedly roared through him. Rage so hot and so bitter it burned in his blood. "Everybody sees what Peter did. Even I do."

He fought the hatred for the brother he'd always loved, but it boiled like a witch's cauldron. The thing he didn't want to acknowledge burst inside him, refusing to be ignored. Even though Peter saved Dominic from their own dad, nobody had had to save Peter. Their father had loved him.

"But I'm doing both of our jobs now. Peter was an ace. No question about it. At one job. I'd like to see *him* do both." He turned to the door. "Drink your cocoa before it gets cold."

Slapping his hands on the swinging door, he strode through, not allowing himself to finish the conversation in his mind. He didn't want to be angry with Peter. He had adored his brother. He didn't want to be suffocating under the weight of his life. But he was. He wasn't called to do this. His dad had told him time and again he was meant to be the guy on the sidelines. Second best. So he'd adjusted.

And now he couldn't do the things Peter did with ease, which was why he didn't want to raise Peter's son. He wanted to watch *Peter* enjoy the little boy he'd brought into the world. He wanted to see *Peter* slowly introduce Joshua to the business that was the family heritage. He wanted everything to go back to the way it was. And nothing Audra could say would change that. He was done hearing her try.

But she scrambled through the door right behind him. "Don't run when you're finally getting to the truth!"

He whirled to face her, so angry heat emanated from him. "What I think you're missing is that this is none of your business."

"And what I think *you're* missing is that I understand exactly what you're telling me. The real bottom line is that you feel inadequate."

"And you understand because you felt inadequate when you were left at the altar?" he mocked.

But it didn't deter her. Instead she stepped into his space again, crowding him, confronting him, forcing him to face demons he wanted to pretend didn't exist. "What else do you think I would feel? Basically, the man I loved told me I wasn't good enough. What we had wasn't important. Having children with me wasn't an incentive to settle down."

Their situations were worlds apart. It amazed him she couldn't see that. "That's not how to look at it, Audra. He wasn't running from you. He simply couldn't let go of his lifestyle because it's who he was."

"Oh, yeah? Then why'd he marry somebody else?"

For a few seconds Dominic absorbed that, because it didn't make sense. Try as he might to reassemble the words or think through the concepts to find the inherent logic, he couldn't force it to make sense. "He married somebody else?"

"Yes. And he bought a big house in the country. And according to our mutual friends he's in wedded bliss." That was the part that hurt Audra the most. She could see David marrying somebody on a whim. She could also see him buying a huge mansion to play house with the new "love" in his life. But when she heard through the grapevine that he loved his new life and wanted children, a knife had twisted in her heart. David wasn't afraid of marriage. He simply hadn't wanted to be married to her.

She took a cleansing breath and stepped back, away from Dominic. "Sorry."

"No, I'm sorry." His voice softened.

"Don't be." She tried to muster some righteous indignation so she could at least appear strong. She couldn't. Instead she licked her lips and forged on — for Joshua. "We're both in the same boat. You feel inadequate because you can't do all the jobs thrust on you and you have to listen to people praise your brother, knowing his load was lighter. I feel inadequate because my fiancé left me, then married someone sort of like me but different enough to make me feel I could have been her if I had tried just a little bit harder."

She swallowed. Told herself to move off her fiancé and get back to Joshua. But the suffocating sense of inadequacy couldn't be shaken, and, being with someone who understood, she longed to just let it all out.

Dominic stepped close again. "Whoever your fiancé was, he was an ass."

Audra laughed in spite of herself. "Don't. You don't have to make fun of him to make me feel better."

"No. I don't. You're a smart, beautiful woman. You most certainly don't need a man who didn't appreciate that."

Sliding his hand under the hair at her nape, he pulled her an inch closer and angled her head so he could kiss her.

When his lips touched hers, the breath

froze in Audra's lungs, the blood in her veins stopped moving. He slanted his mouth over hers, coaxing her back to life, and everything inside her seemed to melt with longing. Her hands slid up his arms, absorbing the smooth feel of his tux and stopped on his shoulders as he nudged her against him.

Though Audra had genuinely believed she shouldn't get involved with him, the pieces of his life — his personality — that he'd shown her tonight caused her to reconsider that. He might seem like the prince in the ivory tower she had believed him to be, but he was actually a real person, and she was tasting him, holding him. And from his kiss she could tell he didn't merely consider her the woman caring for his child. She was a person, too. There was more between them than the job she held in his life. They had a connection.

But just when the kiss would have become interesting, would have passed the boundary from emotional to sexual, Dominic pulled away. He stared at her for a few seconds and then took a step back.

Gazing into her eyes, he said, "Sorry."

Audra took a breath. Not quite sure what to say. Suddenly everything between them was different.

But she didn't have to say anything. Dominic had turned and left her standing alone in the silent corridor.

CHAPTER EIGHT

Audra felt the air virtually crackle when Dominic entered the nursery the next morning. One simple kiss had changed everything. They'd connected when they both knew they shouldn't have. He'd said he wasn't going to flirt with her anymore, but when they'd talked openly and honestly about things they couldn't tell anybody else, he hadn't had to flirt. They'd connected and he hadn't been able to help kissing her.

Worse, she kept getting signals that she'd misjudged him. Not only did he at least try to be in Johsua's life when his time was so limited, but also he worried he couldn't be a good father because he didn't have an example to follow. From the way he agonized over his new roles for his family, there was clearly more to him than there had been to David. Categorizing him with her ex suddenly seemed horribly inappropriate.

He set two mugs of coffee on the dresser

by the changing table, and took Joshua from her arms.

"Okay. I might not like what you said to me last night. But I heard it." He glanced around the nursery as if seeing it for the first time. "Even though I have no idea how to be a dad, I do love him." He caught her gaze. "Already."

She smiled, her heart swelling with affection for him and the renewed belief that he was nothing like her ex. "That's great."

He snorted a laugh. "Yeah, we'll see how great it is as I fumble my way through the morning routine." He took a breath. "What do I do?"

"Undress him while I put water in his tub. Then we can bathe him and get him ready for the day." She paused. "Unless you feel comfortable enough to play with him while I shower first?"

His dour mood instantly fled. A devilish smile lifted his lips. "Sure. Go ahead. Strip for your shower."

It was meant to be a joke, but the air between them crackled and then turned thick and heavy. This time more than chemistry arched between them. She'd kissed him. She liked him. And he liked her.

Still, this wasn't the time to do anything about it. Joshua's needs had to come first.

"There are ten bathrooms in this house if there's one." She tried to say it firmly but her voice came out soft, breathy. "If you get any ideas, I can simply carry my clothes to another room."

Shaking his head, he turned away. "All right. Go shower. I won't peek."

But she knew he'd heard the catch in her voice, a dead giveaway of what she felt. He could have pressed, forced her to admit it, but he didn't have to. Her feelings had woven into her breathy voice. And being in the same house meant there would be other times — times when they'd be alone. When Joshua was asleep. Would they be able to pretend there was nothing between them then?

Did she really want to?

Pushing that worry to the back of her mind for later, she said, "You're sure you'll be okay with the baby?"

"As long as you don't take a two-hour shower."

She laughed at the ridiculousness of that, then unexpectedly realized his parents had probably never timed his showers after getting a huge water bill, the way her mother had. And something important struck her. Each understood the other's loss, but neither understood the other's normal life.

"I won't take long. I'll also change his diaper before I go. All you'll have to do is entertain him while I'm gone."

Audra quickly changed Joshua's diaper and gave him back to Dominic. Racing through her bedroom, she grabbed clean underwear from the top dresser drawer and the sunny-yellow nightshirt from the stash Dominic had bought her.

She showered, slipped into the panties, bra and nightshirt, and then dried her hair before she padded into the sitting room where Dominic sat on the rocker watching the morning news as Joshua chewed his plastic pretzel.

Standing in the doorway, she said, "See, that wasn't so bad."

He turned to look at her and smiled. "Hey, yellow's a really good color for you."

"Thanks." But butterflies had taken wing in her tummy. He didn't even have to flirt with her anymore for her to feel the breathless attraction. Just being in the same room with him sent her senses reeling. Yet, at the same time, she was oddly comfortable with him. Or maybe accustomed to him was a better word. They'd gone from totally misinterpreting each other, to arguing, to being comfortable in a little over a week. Comfortable, yet attracted . . . like a couple?

She suddenly wondered if this was how their morning routine would unfold if they were dating. If they were to pursue the attraction, there would be times she would sleep over. Would they check in on the baby? Or actually handle the morning routine together? Since she'd spent time as Joshua's nanny, it seemed only natural that they'd slide into the nursery and get the little boy once they woke.

The picture she imagined filled her with such a sense of rightness that she had to shake her head to chase it away.

Because it was wrong. She kept looking at Dominic and his life through *her* experiences, but as her mother had reminded her, his real life was nothing like the world she knew. A wealthy man like Dominic wouldn't do baby chores. He'd leave that for a nanny. He would come into the nursery to hold the clean, dry, fed, happy baby. Changing the baby and feeding it after its night's sleep would never be part of Dominic's morning routine.

And she couldn't imagine having a child and letting his care go to a non family member. Not even for a night or a morning of sleeping in.

"So, are you ready to bathe him?"

"Whenever you are."

She filled the baby tub while he undressed Joshua. As if in perfectly synchronized choreography, they slid the baby into the tub, passed soap and a washcloth back and forth, shampooed his hair, rinsed him, rolled him in his towel and took him to the changing table.

Watching Dominic wrestle the squirming, happy baby, Audra's heart twisted in her chest. If he could simply commit, forget that he could afford a nanny, using hired care only for the times he couldn't be home, and do the job like a normal single dad, he would be a wonderful father.

"I'm going out of town tonight."

He said the words quietly, hesitantly, and Audra's heart twisted again. His life came with too many pressures, too many responsibilities to be a real dad. And no matter how sad it was for Joshua to face a future of being raised by nonfamily, she needed to accept that Dominic's life was different and quit pushing him.

"I have to leave right after dinner, but I thought maybe . . . you know . . . we could, um . . . take Joshua somewhere when I get home."

"What do you mean take him somewhere?"

"He's stuck in the house all the time, so I

thought maybe we should take him some-where . . . change his scenery."

Dominic might not have time to be a normal dad, but with a simple suggestion he had melted her heart. Wanting to take the baby out was the most adorable thing she'd ever heard. He was thinking. Trying. Proving that deep down he had what it took to be a good daddy.

"Well," she said hesitantly, "if you want to change his scenery, all we have to do is explore this house. We could show him a different room every day and not get back to the first one until next month."

Dominic laughed. "I'd actually like to take him out of the house."

His genuine laughter touched her soul more than any of his flirting ever could have. The longer they were together, the more the real Dominic emerged. He wasn't the flippant playboy he liked people to believe he was. *This* was the real Dominic Manelli. That was why their time together kept getting more and more difficult.

Their eyes met over the changing table, and Audra's breath stuttered in her chest. She'd never denied that his chiseled features and perfect physique attracted her. She'd also never denied that his sense of humor and fun called to a part of her that no one else seemed to care existed. But now he was adding another dimension to his attractiveness. He was revealing his real personality. There was no greater show of trust.

Desperately trying not to make too much of that, she lowered her gaze. "Special time with Joshua is a great idea. Even getting him outside is a great idea. But, again, you don't need to go any farther than your backyard."

"That doesn't sound like a whole lot of fun."

"It will be for Joshua. He just wants time with you. He doesn't care where. You don't have to spend money or buy him gifts." She stepped back as he lifted the baby from the changing table. "It's supposed to be sunny on Saturday. We could simply take a walk through the grounds and get some fresh air."

He turned from the table, baby on his arm. Though his initial hesitancy was gone, he still appeared out of his element. As if he didn't quite trust himself yet.

"Every day it's going to get easier."

He smiled uncertainly. "Right."

"I'm serious."

He said, "Uh-huh," as he leaned over and handed Joshua to her. Forearms brushed, fingers touched, and memories of the kiss the night before washed over her.

With their faces inches apart, he said, "I'll

miss you while I'm gone."

His nearness had always been overwhelming, but now she'd kissed him. He hadn't just kissed her. She'd kissed him back. There was no pretending she didn't feel something. She swallowed. "I'll miss you, too."

He pulled away with a laugh. "That's the first concession I've had from you."

She might not be able to pretend she didn't feel anything, but that didn't mean she'd revert to old habits. A relationship between them wouldn't work. Even if he wasn't the playboy at heart he pretended to be, they came from two different worlds. Another lesson she'd learned from David, albeit after the fact. David's new wife came from old money. When he'd really settled down, he'd settled with one of his own kind.

Even if she and Dominic fit together perfectly, she didn't fit in his life. The house manager's daughter with the millionaire owner?

No.

She wouldn't be foolish a second time. This time she would save herself a lot of heartache by just not letting anything happen between her and Dominic.

Busying herself with adjusting Joshua on her arm, she said, "I've gotta go." She headed for the door. "If I don't get him to my mom soon so I can get dressed for work, I'll be late."

"Not going to let me kiss you goodbye?"

The unexpected offer of another kiss stopped her where she stood. But another kiss was wrong for so many reasons even the thought was ridiculous. So ridiculous that maybe his question was intended to be silly. Foolish. Just fun. Just flirting. Not real.

She took a breath, tipped her head sideways and smiled. "No."

He laughed. "Right. At least let me kiss Joshua."

He stepped over, placed one hand on Joshua's back and balanced the other on Audra's shoulder. Leaning in, he pressed a soft kiss to Joshua's round, pink cheek, and Joshua squealed with delight.

Over the baby's head, Dominic caught her gaze. The odd sensation she'd had when she'd returned from her shower spun a web around her again. The sense of warmth and comfort. The cozy, honest feeling of being a family. Of belonging together.

But instead of being heartened, another terrible realization struck her. Neither she nor Dominic was Joshua's natural parent, but the three of them were bonding. Not just Dominic and Joshua. Not just her and

Dominic. But the three of them. Almost like family. She knew Dominic felt it, too, when his eyes narrowed and he pulled away. That was only going to make it harder for all of them when she left.

Yet another reason to keep her distance. If she didn't watch what happened between them in the time she spent at Dominic's home, they would form a family of sorts and then Joshua would lose another "mom and dad."

But how would she avoid the man she was living with, the man she ate dinner with, the man who needed the boost of confidence she gave him when he was with the baby?

She wouldn't. So maybe the real solution was to make him see just how wrong they were for each other so that he became as cautious around her as she intended to be around him.

That night when Dominic came home, Audra was waiting at the door with Joshua. "Good evening."

He shrugged out of his top coat. "Good evening."

"Wanna take him?"

Though he was tired, Dominic had to admit it was nice to see the fresh face of his happy nephew. He smiled slightly. The kid

129

wouldn't be in a good mood every night, so this might be the only chance he got to do the right thing when it was easy. Besides, he was leaving in a few hours. He would be gone even before it was time to put Joshua to bed.

"Sure."

He took the baby, and Audra led him into the dining room. "I had Joyce make fettuccine Alfredo for you tonight."

"You know my favorite food?"

She laughed. "I asked."

Her laughter broke the stupor of his exhaustion like a ray of sun dissipating fog. He walked to his seat at the head of the table. "You know this stuff is a heart attack on a plate."

She leaned toward him and whispered, "One night won't hurt."

"Luckily, I have a treadmill in my office."

She laughed again but Dominic saw the high chair beside his place at the table and froze. The last time he'd tried to put Joshua in the high chair he'd made a mess of things.

Before he could say anything, Audra reached over and took the baby from his arms. "I know you probably want to let him sit on your lap, but he'd have his fingers in your food at some point and I think that could get a little messy."

Dominic breathed an internal sigh of relief. "Thank you."

"Hey, it's my job to make your life easier."

He chuckled. Funny how she hadn't noticed that before. Or had she? When he really thought about it, she'd been the one to do all the baby duty, except if he volunteered. When she pressed him, it was only to get him to spend time with his nephew.

He took a breath. Audra seated herself and said, "How was your day?"

"Exhausting."

"Are you ready for your trip out of town?"

"Barely."

She laughed. "We're not going to have much of a conversation, if you don't say more than one-word answers."

If she hadn't laughed when she'd said it, Dominic might have felt pressured. Instead he relaxed. "You're right."

"Two words!"

This time he laughed. "What do you want to talk about?"

"I like hearing about your life."

"Right."

"I'm serious. You come from an entirely different kind of world than I do. Your approach to everything is different. Even our thought processes don't work the same. What's commonplace to you would probably be interesting to me."

His brow furrowed. "Is that how you see me?"

"Isn't that how you see me? As somebody from another world? Somebody different."

"No. I just see you as a person."

She laughed merrily. "Probably because you're not privy to the inside of my life the way I am yours because I'm living at your house."

He inclined his head. "Makes sense. So what would I see if I went into your house?"

"First of all, it's an apartment. Small. Bright. Not much there. But if you went with me to work, you'd really see the difference between our stations in life. I have a boss. She owns Wedding Belles. Four of my friends do the actual wedding planning. We have an assistant, Julie."

"The one getting married?"

She nodded and smiled, obviously pleased he'd remembered the detail. "And then there's me. I'm the background person."

"You're their accountant. You're hardly background."

"Really? Is your accountant out front?"

"Yes! He's our chief financial officer and he's even on the board —"

"Maybe in a bigger company the guy who manages the money is high profile, but not a little one."

"Your function is still important."

"I know that. I'm just saying that's another difference between us. You're an out-front person. I'm background."

"Ah, so that's what this is all about. You're showing me how different we are because of that kiss."

She blushed. "Did it work?"

"No." Yes. Not because he wasn't interested but because he suddenly saw how he could hurt her. She had met him at the door with a happy baby, had the cook prepare his favorite meal and joined him for dinner, not for any reason but to be kind, considerate. She was a sweet person. And he liked her. It was hard not to. He wanted to spend time with her, date her, probably even sleep with her. But that's all he wanted. Once their affair had run its course, he wouldn't exactly toss her aside. But his calls and invitations would slow until eventually they stopped. And she would be hurt. Very hurt.

Only a complete idiot couldn't see that; and only a complete bastard would pursue her knowing he'd ultimately hurt her.

He tossed his napkin to the table and rose. "You know what? I think I'll get my things together and go. Thank Joyce for the wonderful dinner, but I really don't have time to eat."

Dominic used the day he was away to strengthen his resolve about keeping his distance from Audra. But when he returned from his trip on Friday night, just the sight of her undid all his hard work. His heart lurched in his chest and he felt more alive than he had the entire time he'd been gone. He didn't realize how lonely he'd been until he experienced how good it was to have someone to come home to.

She, unfortunately, seemed to believe that he was happy to see Joshua, and handed the baby to him as soon as his topcoat was removed.

He *was* happy to see the baby, and gratified that the little guy seemed very glad to see him. Not just because it took his attention off his feelings for Audra, but because it proved he was making progress in being a good dad.

"Hey, there, little man."

The baby screeched and hollered, slapping Dominic's cheeks with his chubby hands.

"He's been moody the whole time you were gone."

"Really?"

Audra laughed. The joyful expression in

her eyes filled him with pride. She was thrilled he and Joshua were bonding, and anything that pleased her pleased him.

"Yes. I could tell he missed you. He'd probably like nothing better than to play, but it's time for him to go to bed."

"I'll get him ready." The words popped out of his mouth naturally, but once they were out, Dominic didn't regret them. He could do this. Thanks to Audra. "Why don't you watch TV in the entertainment room . . . or make yourself some cocoa?"

"Really?"

"Yeah." He stepped back, away from her. It felt wrong to exclude her. He loved having her in the room with them, even if he did the baby things himself. Yet he didn't want to hurt her.

"You want to do a solo flight?"

He nodded, backing away again. "Yes." His needs didn't matter. Hers did. She'd done so much for him that he couldn't hurt her.

The next morning when Dominic got out of bed, he immediately made the trip to the nursery to say good-morning. Determined to keep his distance, he put his focus on Joshua. But the baby was in a frisky mood and he splashed and played, causing Audra to laugh. The sound seeped into him, making him feel silly and wonderful. At ease in a way he hadn't felt in a long, long time.

"What are you doing?" he asked, tickling the baby who squealed with delight, slapping his chubby palms on the water and splashing Dominic. He tickled the baby again. "Is this war?"

The baby giggled. Audra laughed, too. Unable to stop himself, he looked over his shoulder at her and his heart just about stopped. She looked so perfect standing behind him cheering him on.

She also looked happy. Normal. Not stiff and formal as she had been when he'd first hired her. Not afraid, as she'd been when he'd flirted. Not determined when forced to confront him about spending time with the baby. But normal.

As if she were right where she belonged.

The vision froze the breath in his lungs. He couldn't help thinking this was the way his life was supposed to be, even though he knew that wasn't true. He didn't want this life. He wanted his old life back. But he also knew he wasn't going to get it, and he wondered — no he *worried* — that he was seeing comfort and perfection in her simply because his other options had been snatched away from him.

He pulled Joshua from the tub and handed

him off to Audra, who stood waiting with a towel. "I've got some work to do in the den this morning."

She smiled cheerfully. "Sure. No problem. Go now."

Don't be nice to me. He almost said it out loud. *Protect yourself. I need somebody and you're available and if you let me, I'll hurt you.*

Instead he said, "Thanks," and all but ran from the room. She was simply too tempting. But he was all wrong for her, and he didn't know how to fix the problem of liking her more every time they were together. Except to stay away from her.

When Audra brought the baby in to him an hour later — when he was in the middle of writing summaries of his meetings from the day he was out of town — it was very easy to get himself out of spending more time with her.

"All right. We both agree I need to be with the baby, but we're going to have to set some limits." He closed the lid of his laptop. "Especially when I have work to do."

She grimaced. "You're busy. Sorry. I just thought you'd said you wanted to take him somewhere today."

She was so genuinely nice that he forgave himself for the feelings he was developing for her. He'd have to be a monk not to like her. But that only made it all the more important that he stay away from her.

"No. *I'm* sorry. I did say that, but I said it before I realized I would have so much work to do."

"Maybe you can spend some time with him this afternoon?"

He said, "Maybe," only to get her out of his office. He wouldn't have any more time that afternoon than he did right now, but he didn't want to argue and he knew the danger of spending too much time with her. He was simply beginning to like her too much and had grown too accustomed to having her around. Still, the pressure of the lie felt like a vise around his temple.

To salve his conscience, he worked through lunch, desperate to get everything done, to have time for Joshua. When he realized he was making time for Joshua to please Audra, he ran his hands down his face. Liking her, being kind to her, wanting to be with her was wrong, because he knew himself. In the end he would hurt her.

But it felt so darned right. She was sweet and beautiful and he liked her. Every instinct screamed that he should at the very least give a relationship between them a shot. But he really wasn't the kind of guy to settle down, and in spite of what he'd told her when she first came to work for him, after getting to know her, he now realized she did need the kind of man who would marry her.

The phone on the desk buzzed. Rather than let one of the overworked weekend staff grab it, Dominic did. "Manelli."

"Hey, Dom!"

Dominic sat back on his tall-back desk chair, recognizing the voice as Tom Jenson's. Tom had been a "business" friend of Peter's, who by default had become a friend of Dominic's.

"Hey, Tom, what's up?"

"I'm having some people over this afternoon to watch the basketball game."

Because he'd rushed through his work, he was done. But he'd hurried to have time to spend with Joshua. "Sorry. I can't."

"Really? That's too bad, because Alfred Longoria is going to be here."

"*The* Alfred Longoria?"

"*The* Alfred Longoria. Internet mogul. Darned near the smartest guy on the planet. And you'll get three hours of hooting and hollering and drinking and just plain being a guy with him."

Which was why Tom had called him. He knew Dominic was in trouble implementing Peter's Internet-expansion plan. If Tom helped Dominic on this, Dominic would help him the next time he needed a favor.

"And if I come over and join you, then I can probably run Peter's plan by him and see where we're making our mistake."

"Exactly."

"Be there in twenty minutes."

Dominic grabbed a jacket and left. He didn't give a thought to Joshua or Audra until the game was over and most of the guys had jumped out of their seats and headed for their coats and cars. Wives and kids were waiting for them.

Dominic half rose, guilt surfacing for the first time that afternoon. He had a temporary nanny and a baby boy who didn't even know where he'd gone. He'd run because he was afraid of what he was beginning to feel for Audra. But he'd also come to Tom's to see Alfred Longoria and he hadn't even had a chance to talk to him. Wouldn't it kill two birds with one stone to stay a bit longer?

"What'll it be, Al?" Tom asked, heading for the bar. "Another beer or your coat?"

"I'm not in any hurry to get home," Alfred said, laughing before he chugged the remainder of the beer he held. "So make it a beer."

The thrill of an opportunity raced through Dominic and he sat down again.

Then Alfred added, "I could kick myself for not letting my lawyer draw up a prenup."

And Dominic knew now was not the time to bring up his Internet-expansion problems.

"Trouble in paradise?" Tom asked as he rounded the bar and approached the seating arrangement with three beers.

"Hell, yeah," Alfred said as Tom passed two brown bottles to Dominic and Alfred. "My wife likes the money. She just doesn't want me to work."

Dominic had heard his father scream a version of those words to his mother so many times that they still sent a rush of fear through him. His mother also had been a disappointment to his dad. He didn't need a therapist to tell him that was another reason he'd never tried to be like his dad, why he paid little or no attention to him. Why he didn't have a clue how to raise a child or run a business.

Ed Nevel emerged from the hall bathroom off Tom's basement retreat. He grabbed his jacket from the rack by the bar. "Hey, Dom, I'm going to Shady Hady's tonight. Wanna come with? Erin's going to be there."

Dominic and Erin had been Boston's hot couple in the weeks before Peter's death. And by *hot* he didn't merely mean popular.

From the second they'd met they hadn't been able to keep their hands off each other. Yet he hadn't even thought of her in weeks. Tonight, when he did remember her, he felt nothing. "Thanks, but no, thanks."

Alfred groaned. "Oh, come on. You've got a hot woman waiting for you at a club and you don't want to go?"

Visions of his awkward nights out, not having a good time but feeling trapped, filled Dominic's head.

"No."

But even as he declined the offer, Dominic regretted it. He didn't exactly want to see Erin, but he needed a night out. He needed some fun. No, he didn't need "fun" per se. The truth was he was lonely. Alone. Tired of being all by himself in a house with twenty or thirty servants and no one to talk to.

Except Audra. Maybe that's why they were developing feelings for each other that were all wrong.

Ed shook his head. "Whatever, Dom. See you around."

Tom said, "See you around, Ed."

As Ed disappeared up the stairs, Tom skillfully directed the conversation to Manelli Holdings' failing plan to launch three new Internet sites. In his element, Alfred rattled off six or eight reasons the plan was in trouble, as well as six or eight good ideas Dominic and his team hadn't thought of. They debated all the angles. Almost completely revised Dominic's simplistic impression of a very complicated enterprise and suddenly it was nine o'clock.

Alfred bounced off the couch, reaching for his cell phone. "Oh, crap. I'm going to be shot. By now Stella's home. She's tried on her purchases, had two glasses of wine and is getting angrier by the second that I'm not home." He hit a speed-dial number and called his driver.

Dominic said, "Blame me. It was the discussion of my business that kept you."

"Screw that," Alfred replied, shrugging into his coat. "I should be allowed to have a day out without having to explain myself."

Tom muttered something sympathetic and then led Dominic and Alfred up the stairs to the foyer of Tom's stunning home. The front door opened and Mabel Fortune, Tom's long-time girlfriend, walked in.

"Oh-oh." Mabel shook her long red hair off her face and it rippled down her back. "Guys' afternoon not over?"

Tom kissed her cheek hello. "We're clearing out now."

Mabel displayed the two grocery bags on

her arms. "Too late for supper?"

"How about if I cook you breakfast?"

She laughed. "Sounds promising. I'll put these away and see you upstairs." She glanced at Dominic and Alfred. "Nice to see you both."

Dominic and Alfred mumbled something appropriate, watching Mabel as she walked down the hall and disappeared. Alfred's cell phone buzzed, announcing his driver, and within seconds Alfred was also gone.

Dominic said good-night and he, too, left. But on the way to his car, he realized something so important that he sat without saying a word while his driver took him home.

Ed was a player. He had time. He had money. He could do what he wanted when he wanted. With whom he wanted. But with a baby to raise and a business to run, that option had gone for Dominic.

Alfred was miserable. Married to a woman who probably didn't work and had too much time on her hands, who wanted Alfred to entertain her. Just as Dominic's parents had been before his dad had retired to Florida.

But Tom was happy. He and Mabel — a lawyer every bit as busy as Tom — were a perfect combination. Neither one of them had time to commit to a marriage any more than they had time to continually jet around, looking for love, sex or even amusement. They were equals. Equally independent, equally busy, equally successful, they clicked sexually . . . and had no time for a family.

Dominic suddenly saw that he was made for a relationship like Tom and Mabel's. And even though Audra was the woman who currently haunted his dreams and made him want to stay home on a night he should have been dying to go out, she wasn't the woman to have that kind of relationship with him. One guy had already hurt her. And she was falling for Dominic. He needed to get his head on straight and do the right thing — leave her alone.

And maybe the way to do that would be to find his own Mabel Fortune?

"Where were you?"

Audra pounced on Dominic the minute he stepped into his foyer. For two seconds he wondered why it had saddened him that he had to stay away from her. Then he looked into her soft blue eyes, saw her ever-present smile and realized she hadn't pounced, he'd simply interpreted it as her hounding him because he didn't want her to be so nice that he fell in love with her.

He shrugged out of his jacket. "I went to a friend's house to watch the game. I'm sorry. I should have told you."

"I probably should scold you, but watching a game with friends sounds like fun."

"Once again it was business."

"I'm sorry."

He snorted a laugh, heading down the hall to the den for a few minutes of privacy before he went to bed. "Once again it's not your fault."

Unfortunately, speaking as he walked encouraged her to follow him.

"No, but you know I don't mind talking about it."

At the last dinner they'd had together she'd seemed determined to point out how different their lives were. He supposed this was an extension of that conversation. Talking about their lives to make sure they both realized they weren't a good match. But they didn't need to continue it. He knew they were worlds apart. He'd made a plan to keep himself from getting too close to her. It wasn't something he could tell her, but it was a done deal. She was safe.

"There's nothing to talk about."

"We could start with why you're sullen when an afternoon with friends should have made you chatty."

Stepping into the den furnished in the same dark brown leather furniture that had been there since he was a child, he burst out laughing. "Men don't get chatty." He strode to a discreet armoire, opened a door revealing the bar and reached for the Scotch. "My dad would have a real field day with you."

She grimaced. "I'm sure he has some redeeming qualities."

"Oh, yeah. He's a peach." He displayed the bottle of Scotch and she declined a drink with a shake of her head. Before she could ask him another question about his life or continue a conversation he didn't care to get into, he said, "So what else do you do at Wedding Belles?"

Not even a bit thrown off by the change of subject, she shrugged. "I told you, all I do is add and subtract and make budgets and forecasts. I'd really like to talk about you."

"No kidding."

"Seriously. I know your life has been hard these past few weeks, and I'm here. Why not talk?"

He drew a breath. Because he didn't want to. Because there was no point. Because every time he talked to her they got a little closer and that was wrong. Because he didn't want to hurt her.

"We could talk about your brother."

"This isn't the time or place."

"You've got to talk about it sometime."

"Not really. My father always said real men don't talk. Especially not about feelings."

"Okay. Now I'm starting to think your dad must be a real piece of work."

She didn't know the half of it. "And he's happily settled in Miami right now. Over a thousand miles away. So there's no point in discussing him."

"Actually, with him that far away I'd think you would feel free to talk."

He laughed. "Huh!"

"Come on. Tell me some stuff about your brother."

"No."

"Why not?"

Because I want so badly to tell you that I know it has to be wrong. "Not tonight."

"You're obviously angry with him. Probably in the anger stage of grief."

He pounded his fist on the bar. "That's enough!"

The sound of his fist echoed in the suddenly silent room.

Audra took a step back. "I'm sorry."

148

Overwhelmed, he ran his fingers through his short hair, spiking it. "No, I'm sorry. I just don't like being pushed."

The sound of Joshua crying filled the office from a monitor somewhere. Dominic hadn't even known they'd installed monitors. Yet another thing she'd done for him because she was good and smart. While he was nothing but bitter and angry and difficult with her.

Audra turned to the door. "He's probably wet. I'll go upstairs and change him."

Dominic grabbed the bottle of Scotch again, not watching her go. But when he knew he was alone, he rubbed his hand across his mouth. Damn it. He was losing his mind. He dropped the Scotch on the bar and ran up the stairs.

When he opened the door to the nursery, Audra was changing Joshua's diaper.

"I was right. He's just wet. He'll probably go back to sleep the second I lay him in the crib."

"Look. There are two really good reasons I don't want to talk about my brother. The first is that I don't want to say unkind things about him."

"I understand."

He ran his hand across the back of his neck. "Audra, you couldn't possibly understand. A few nights ago even you admitted it. Our lives are worlds apart."

"Okay."

"Damn it! Don't be nice to me! Don't forgive me for yelling."

She shook her head. "What do you want me to do? Yell back? Not in front of the baby."

"Right." He blew out his breath harshly. "The thing is my dad pitted me and Peter against each other when we were younger, until Peter was the one who proved himself to be the person suited to run the family conglomerate."

"Wow. Your dad gave you a shot?"

He laughed. "Trust you to find the sunny side of what my dad did. But no. He did not give me a shot. My dad was showing Peter he wasn't a shoo-in just because he was the elder. Unfortunately, to do that he more or less had to humiliate me."

She grimaced, lifting Joshua off the changing table. "Ouch."

"My dad wasn't always nice."

"He was one of those turn-his-boys-into-men kind of dads."

"Exactly." Not at all. His dad had been a cruel disciplinarian. The lucky end result had been that his boys had become men, but that was more because Dominic and

Peter had formed a team. Helped each other. Peter had rescued Dominic, then Dominic had become his right-hand man.

Dominic meandered through the quiet nursery. He picked up a small statue of a bear with its paw in a jar of honey and examined it. "I'm going to stink as a father. My dad was such a bad example of parenting that I seriously don't know how to be a dad."

"But Peter did it."

"Peter could do anything." He turned from the small dresser and caught her gaze. "And I'm not bitter. I loved my brother. I didn't want him to die. I most certainly didn't want to be handed everything he had *earned*. I failed in the competition, so I wasn't trained to do any of this. Peter was. And that's the man, the example Joshua should see."

"But you're doing fine."

He laughed. "I'm the also-ran. Peter was the star, yet every day I'll live with the knowledge that Joshua will never see that. Never know his dad. Never see him or talk to him."

Suddenly tired, he headed for the door, but he stopped and faced her again. "And, yes. I think that's unfair to Joshua."

"Oh, Dominic." She walked over and put

her hands on his lapels. "Joshua won't suffer by knowing you. You're wonderful, too."

She rose to her tiptoes and touched her lips to his. What started off, Dominic was sure, as a simple gesture of approval, turned into something hot and sweet very quickly. Their mouths melded together, their tongues began to twine, their bodies to mold together.

But the very fact that the kiss was so sweet, so genuine, So wonderful, brought Dominic to his senses. This woman was too nice for him, and he needed to leave her alone.

He pulled back and turned away. He walked out of the nursery before she had a chance to compose herself enough to stop him.

Walking into Wedding Belles on Monday morning, Audra thought about that conversation with Dominic — the things that had led to a kiss that she should regret giving him, but didn't.

She couldn't change his overwhelming sense that he was taking Peter's place, but she did understand. Joshua was too young to have memories of Peter. In time, with Dominic taking over the role as daddy, it would be as if Peter had never existed.

She entered the foyer, poised to say good-morning to Julie, but Julie wasn't at her desk. The unexpected quiet of the usually bustling foyer allowed her to hear the low hum of activity in the other rooms.

Walking back down the hall to the steps, she heard the delighted gasp of a bride as she saw her gown for the first time. She could picture Serena stepping back, enjoying the moment. Gowns were Serena's art.

Closer to the kitchen, she smelled the raspberry drizzle before she heard the groan of appreciation as a bride or a mother of the bride took her first taste of one of Natalie's decadent wedding cake samples. That made her smile.

But at the bottom of the steps, Audra paused. She smelled Callie's flowers. Was surrounded by wedding photos that hung on the walls to give brides examples of what Regina could do with a camera.

She was immersed in the beauty of artists dedicated to creating the perfect wedding. Was it any wonder she'd expected a proposal from David?

She climbed the steps and walked to her office deep in thought. When she pushed open the door, Julie glanced up from the second desk. "Hey, good morning, Audra!"

"Julie?"

"I'm taking tomorrow off, so I'm getting a jump on invoices today."

"Oh. Great." Audra shrugged out of her coat. "Got special plans?"

Julie jerked her gaze away from the computer screen as if she were surprised by Audra's question. "Hmm?"

"Plans? Are you doing something special on your day off?"

"Oh. Plans." She shook her head. "No. Not really." She returned her attention to the invoices on the desk. "I just want a few days to myself."

"Tell me about it." As Audra lowered herself to her wonderful beige suede chair, she felt the familiar sense of control return. Work was what she knew. What she was good at. But as much as she loved being busy, she could see that adding her nanny job into the mix had drained her. "After the taxes are filed, I'm going somewhere."

Julie looked up. "Oh, yeah? Where?"

Audra leaned her elbow on her desk and her chin on her closed fist. "I'm thinking somewhere tropical."

Julie mimicked her pose, elbow on her desk, chin on her fist, a faraway look in her eyes. "Somewhere so hot a bathing suit seems like too much clothing and where the ocean is so clear you can see to the bottom."

"Yes."

Even Audra heard the desperation in her own voice and wasn't surprised when Julie laughed. "Girlfriend, I think you should be online making travel arrangements."

"Can't."

"Why not! You sound like you're going to snap."

Thanking God she had a legitimate excuse that kept her from having to explain her exhaustion, Audra said, "I'm still working on Wedding Belles' income taxes."

"Oh, come on. Don't tell me you can't take a weekend off."

"I can't."

"Surely one tax return can't take that long —" Julie's eyes widened, and then she gasped. "You're moonlighting!"

The red of embarrassment seeped into Audra's cheeks. "Moonlighting?"

"You're doing taxes on the side! That's why you're so stressed."

Liking that excuse, Audra didn't really confirm or deny it. "You know I have other clients."

"Audra, you're just so on the ball." Julie turned to the computer again, put her fingers on the keyboard and began inputting invoice information, though she didn't stop talking. "I wish I were like you."

"I wish I were like you." The words popped out of Audra's mouth before she even knew they were forming. But once they were out, Audra didn't want to take them back. "You're so trusting. You're so open. Anything to do with people is so easy for you."

Julie faced Audra, a shadow passing over her face, but before Audra really had a chance to analyze it, Julie grinned. "People are easy. Taxes are hard."

Audra laughed. "To a CPA taxes are easy and people are hard!"

"Nah, you just have to figure out what makes a person tick and then work with that."

Audra tilted her head to one side. "What makes a person tick?"

"For instance, you like logic. So if I need you to do something for me, I appeal to your sense of logic. Callie likes adventure, so when I need something from her I try to make it sound exciting."

Audra laughed. "And with Belle you appeal to her sense of family."

"Exactly."

Tapping her pencil on her desk blotter, Audra thought about Dominic. "What would you do with a guy who is raising his brother's son and afraid the little boy will never know his dad?"

At Julie's confused frown, Audra added, "My mom works for Dominic Manelli."

"The guy you used to chase around at Christmas parties when you were a little girl?" Julie said, smiling at Audra. "You spilled those beans after your third margarita the one and only time you got truly drunk with us."

"I told you about Dominic?"

"Just some basics about what a hottie he is."

"Well, now he's a hottie with a baby to raise."

"And you care because?"

"Because getting control of his family's business was hard enough for him. When he also got custody of his brother's son, he began to feel he was living his brother's life."

"He doesn't want the little boy?"

"He *does* want the little boy. Every time they're together I see that. But he's grieving for his brother. He's overwhelmed with the family business. And on top of that, he feels guilty for taking over his brother's life. He knows that Joshua's never going to remember his dad. And believes Peter deserves to have his son know him."

Julie's face softened. "Wow."

"I don't know how to get him around this or over it or through it." And though it wasn't part of her job as nanny, something inside her couldn't stand to see Dominic so unhappy. Couldn't stand that he didn't see his own goodness because it was blocked by guilt.

Julie shrugged. "Sometimes time is the only thing that gets a person through. Look at you. This is the first man I've heard you talk about since David. And that was almost a year ago."

Audra again felt her face redden. Dominic was the first guy she'd even talked about in a year? "It's not like that."

Julie laughed. "Of course it is. You might not like that you're interested in him, but you are."

Well, sure, she was "interested." He was hot. Deep down inside, he was good. But he didn't want anything permanent. He only wanted to have some fun with her.

She frowned. Was that her only reason for not getting involved with him? Because it suddenly seemed odd that she was refusing to have fun. It was almost as if she was demanding a commitment before she even had a date.

Wow. Was that what she'd done with David? From the first date pressured him into getting serious?

"Don't forget my mother works for him," Audra said, keeping her questions to herself and turning her attention back to the work on her desk, hoping the subject would drop.

"So?"

"What do you mean, 'so?' "

"Audra, I'm not telling you to marry the guy. Lighten up. Have some fun."

Audra swallowed. Apparently she had a reputation for not having fun and demanding commitments.

Julie typed a few things into the computer, then turned to Audra with another sunny smile. "You know, you could talk to Regina about doing some kind of pictorial thing."

"A what?"

"Like a video scrapbook for this Dominic guy. You say he feels guilty because of taking over his brother's life." She caught Audra's gaze. "Solving his business troubles is out of my league, but if you want to ease his guilt a bit about taking over as the baby's new dad, have your mother gather some pictures, and let Regina put a video together. Then give the CD to Dominic."

Audra's mouth dropped open slightly. "If the video was done properly, Joshua would always have his parents with him. Not his real flesh-and-blood parents, but enough of them through pictures and videos that he'd *know* them."

"Exactly."

"And though Dominic would function as Joshua's real dad, he wouldn't 'replace' Peter."

"Nope."

"And he could stop feeling guilty."

"Yep."

Audra popped out of her seat. "Julie, you are a genius."

"Regina is the genius. You get her the pictures. She'll make a CD that will give Joshua his parents, lessen Dominic's sense that he's replacing his brother and maybe free him up enough that you can swoop in and steal his heart."

"I don't want to steal his heart," Audra said automatically. But suddenly she wondered if that was true. If she stopped thinking in terms of commitment or marriage, Dominic was exactly the kind of guy she *should* date. Someone who would show her a good time. Someone she could relax with. Somebody she liked enough to really be herself.

Hadn't he been saying that all along?

The following Saturday Dominic took

Joshua outside for a walk around the grounds, making good on his promise to get the baby out of the house. Though he had expected Audra to join them, she breezily refused, telling him they would be fine and she needed a few minutes to get some work done.

Stepping outside, technically into his own backyard, Dominic felt a little silly, but only two minutes down the path he really looked at his own property and was amazed by how much beauty surrounded him.

"I really never was one for snow," he told Joshua as they walked along a stone path. Sunlight glistened off the small drifts. The gardens were knee-deep in sparkling white snow. Benches coated with frosty white.

"Now, your parents. They were the snow freaks. I like to ski, but they loved to ski."

He stopped. Pain twisted his heart. He could see Peter and Marsha waving from a lift, posing before shoving off and racing down a hill.

"You'll never know that. I'll teach you to ski." He laughed. "Probably badly because I'm not that good. Not like your parents." Getting his mind off Peter and Marsha and what he couldn't do, Dominic changed the subject. "What I can teach you is blackjack. I'm not going to be much help with schoolwork or baseball, but, kid, when you turn twenty-one, I will show you the time of your life."

Guilt invaded again. The only thing he could say for certain that he could do well was take his nephew to Vegas and teach him to gamble. He was about to do a second-rate job in a role Peter would have aced.

Joshua slapped his cheeks.

"I know. You want attention. I already figured out that if I think too much when I'm with you, you'll slap me."

The baby giggled.

Dominic laughed. God, he was a mess. Missing his brother. Wishing he could handle all his jobs as well as Peter would have. And alone.

Except for Audra. Who was off-limits. Because she deserved more, better, than him. In fact, now that he was getting along so well with Joshua it was time to end the temptation.

She hadn't yet worked the full month, but that was okay. He could not only care for Joshua in a pinch, but he also knew what to look for in a new nanny. He could call a service this afternoon and have a temporary at his home by nightfall. Then he and Mary could begin looking for someone permanent.

There was no sense delaying the inevitable. Audra should leave.

CHAPTER NINE

When Dominic stepped into the foyer, Mary met him. "Let me take the little one."

"Where's Audra?"

"Waiting for you. She asked me to get Joshua out of his snowsuit and to direct you to go back to the entertainment room. She has something to show you."

"In the entertainment room?"

"Hey, I'm just the messenger," Mary said with a laugh, already starting up the winding stairway.

Dominic sighed and headed down the hall. He supposed the entertainment room was as good a place as any to tell her he would be calling an agency and getting the ball rolling to hire a real nanny, freeing her. His heart jerked a bit. He'd be lonely without her. But the new nanny could do all the day-to-day things Joshua needed, and now that Dominic was slipping into his role of dad, he'd do his part, too. There was no sense in Audra staying any longer. And plenty of reason to get her away from him before he couldn't resist temptation.

When he reached the entrance of the entertainment room, he pushed open the double doors. His parents had created the small theater long before video tapes and DVDs had become popular. It was the one nod his dad had made toward family time. Though he hadn't joined them often, he had come along for Christmas movies, played on a real movie screen.

The reminder made Dominic shake his head as he walked into the room, past the pool tables and two rows of modified recliners that faced a large-screen high-definition television that had replaced the old white screen. It reminded him again of why he felt shaky about his parenting abilities. His dad had been a total wash as a father.

Wearing comfortable jeans and a bulky red sweater, Audra stood out like a beacon in the butterscotch, tan and yellow room. "Hey."

"Hey." He motioned around. "What's up?"

"I have something for you. Sit." She waited for him to take the few steps that brought him to the recliner beside hers.

She sat and he reluctantly followed suit.

"Audra, there's something we need to talk about."

"This won't take long. We can talk as soon as we're through with this." She clicked the remote activating the television. "I know one of your biggest worries is that you're taking Peter's place in Joshua's life."

He glanced at her, his gaze catching her blue eyes that were soft with sincerity. Pain shimmered around his heart. He was going to miss her. She was one of the sweetest, kindest people he had ever met. But that was exactly why he was all wrong for her.

"I adored my brother. Joshua would have adored him, too. It's not right that he never gets to meet his dad."

The door at the back of the room opened. Mary slipped inside and hustled down the aisle. Handing Joshua to Dominic, she said, "Here you go."

Audra smiled. "Thanks, Mom."

As Mary scurried out of the room, Audra clicked the remote again.

Dominic suddenly realized he'd been set up. Especially when the wide screen before him displayed a picture of Marsha and Peter on their wedding day, waving out of the limo door. Peter looked strong, capable and incredibly happy. A beautiful bride in white satin and pearls, Marsha had been the picture-perfect mate for him.

Pain seized Dominic's heart, but he ignored it. "What's this?" he asked as he adjusted Joshua on his lap.

"Watch," Audra said, then reached for his free hand. Peter's hospital newborn photo flashed on the screen. Audra's fingers squeezed Dominic's as pictures of Peter as a baby, then a toddler, and then a grade-school child paraded across the screen. But the snapshots quickly changed from those of a little boy to a toothless baby girl.

He turned to Audra. "Marsha?"

Audra nodded. "My mother contacted Marsha's mom and got a boatload of pictures."

Dominic's throat tightened. "She was a cute kid."

"Probably why Joshua is so adorable."

The chuckle that escaped Dominic was heavy with unshed tears. Joshua screeched with unhappiness. Dominic jostled him on his lap, whispering, "Hush." Then he pointed at the screen. "That's your mom and dad."

The baby glanced at the pictures on screen as he'd been directed, but just as quickly turned away and snuggled into Dominic's chest.

Dominic's heart expanded with an amazing thought. Joshua hadn't stopped fussing because of the two people on the screen. The baby had settled because he trusted Dominic.

He looked up at the screen again, once again seeing Peter and Marsha, and his throat tightened. It was obscene that the lives of two people so happy, so in love, so filled with promise had been cut off. The thought tore at him as their baby nestled against Dominic's chest, not even slightly interested in them. But for once Dominic wasn't upset. He was here. To Joshua he was real. His parents weren't even a memory. And maybe that was another thing Audra was trying to show him. Joshua might not have memories, but Dominic did. He remembered so many things about Marsha and Peter — and he had pictures.

Still shots of Peter and Marsha at picnics and parties, boating and barbecuing, gave way to the video of their wedding, and suddenly the two quiet people from the photos had voices. Their laughter at the toast and happy tears as they said goodbye leaving for their honeymoon.

"Peter was a softie," Audra said, her words hushed and solemn.

Dominic swallowed hard, unable to speak. He wanted to say so many things. Things

Joshua should know. Things that would bridge the gap between the living and the dead. But he couldn't speak. His grief was still raw, weeping. He recognized that Audra hadn't merely made these tapes to help Joshua know his parents. She'd made them for Dominic, too. So he could see Peter as a real person, not a god of sorts.

The video had moved on to shots of Peter and Marsha's first house, followed by several Christmases with the family, then Marsha pregnant. Her reverent, hopeful voice as she massaged her tummy, speaking to unborn Joshua, cut through Dominic like a knife and tears spilled from his eyes.

"You shouldn't have done this," he whispered hoarsely.

Audra said nothing, only squeezed his hand.

With every scene the pain cut deeper. Though Dominic wanted to run away from the memories that were overwhelming, he couldn't. Suddenly Marsha was in labor, cursing at Peter for taping her. Dominic couldn't help it. He laughed. "God, she hated that he did this."

"We didn't put the whole birth in." As quickly as Audra said it, the scene changed to a hospital bed and Marsha holding newborn Joshua.

Seeing her, Dominic couldn't control his tears. Pulling his hand out of Audra's, he lowered his face to his palm and sobbed. "No two people wanted a baby like they did."

Audra paused the video. "I easily saw that from the videos." She laid her hand on Dominic's shoulder. "I know this is hard for you, but imagine how Joshua will feel when he's old enough to understand. You don't have to worry that he won't know Peter and Marsha. You don't have to feel you're replacing them. You only need to love Joshua, to be their eyes and ears and hands. To say the words they would have said but can't." She rose from her seat, handing him the remote and several more CDs. "If you watch these with him as he's growing up, you can fill in the blanks. You can tell him the stories no one else knows."

She left Dominic alone in the entertainment room with a handful of CDs and a lifetime of memories. He spent the rest of the day there.

Audra wasn't surprised that she didn't see Dominic after she'd left him in the entertainment room. She suspected he had watched all the CDs. She knew he'd grieved all over again for the brother he missed so terribly that he couldn't put it into words. She knew he wasn't ready for company.

What she didn't know was whether or not he appreciated what she had done or if he thought she'd overstepped her boundaries.

When he arrived in the nursery on Sunday morning, coffee in hand, the solemn look on his face told her nothing.

"Good morning."

He cleared his throat. "Good morning." He handed her a mug of coffee. "Modern technology certainly has changed the way we remember things."

"You say that as if you're not sure it's good."

"It's wonderful for Joshua," he said without hesitation. "But yesterday was hard on me."

"I know. I'm sorry."

"Don't be sorry." He sucked in a breath. "I needed to remember that Peter was just a person. But I also needed to be reminded that I had lots of ways to show Joshua his parents." He caught her gaze. "Many people aren't so lucky."

"No, not everybody has tons of videos and still photos. Your family certainly is camera happy."

He laughed and Audra relaxed. "Yeah, my mom and Peter were insane with the camera." He caught her gaze. "But that was good."

"That was very good," Audra softly agreed.

He pulled in a breath. "So how'd you find the time to organize all that?"

"I didn't. Regina, Wedding Belles' photographer, spent the past few days doing nothing but going over your family's videos and stills. The stills were apparently easy. It's the video that took time. She wanted to put in just the right things to instantly get to the heart of who Peter and Marsha were."

"She did a great job."

"These videos will be good while Joshua's in grade school. Then when he's old enough he can look at all the tapes that Regina didn't use. It will be like interacting with his parents in different ways and new environments."

Dominic nodded. "But there's a bit more to it than showing Joshua Peter's life." He pulled in another long draught of air. "I have to thank you for something else."

She frowned. "Really?"

"Yes. The time you spent here has been as good for me as it has been for Joshua."

She busied herself with gathering a fresh diaper and clean outfit for the baby. "I only taught you a few baby things."

"No, it's more. Audra —"

He paused again and Audra faced him. The expression in his eyes caused her heart to skip a beat. After all the thinking she'd done about her life and turning down casual dates in search of commitment, she felt totally different about him and a possible relationship between them. If he asked her to go out and have fun tonight, she wouldn't tell him no.

She held her breath.

"You make me feel as if my life is important."

Not expecting that, she tilted her head in question. "Your life *is* important."

"No, I'm saying this badly." He paced from the crib to the window and back again. "You make me feel as if the things I do, like raising Joshua, matter more than running the company. More than keeping the Manellis wealthy."

Disappointment rattled through her. Not that she didn't want him to find his way and be happy. She was thrilled for Joshua that Dominic had made a total turn-around and that he felt so much better about his situation. But she had a tightening in her chest. A premonition she sometimes experienced right before bad news.

Telling herself she was being silly, she said,

"That's wonderful."

"You're wonderful."

The band around her heart squeezed again, but this time it was with hope. He did have feelings for her. She knew it in her soul. Still, she'd turned him down and told him no so many times she knew that the next move might have to be hers.

"You know, being here has changed me too. Being left at the altar made me feel I was a wash as a woman."

He walked over to her and put his hands on her shoulders. "That's hardly the case."

"Well, thanks to you I understand that now."

Her words drifted away into silence. With Joshua happily occupied in the crib, the quiet and privacy of their situation settled over Audra. They stood only inches apart. He still had his hands on her shoulders. They'd just admitted they liked and helped each other.

Now?

Their gazes caught and clung. He dipped his head and kissed her, pressing his lips to hers softly, hesitantly, kissing her with such emotion and tenderness that everything inside her stilled. He couldn't hide the intensity of his feelings for her. He knew her now. This wasn't about attraction or chemistry. This kiss was about genuine emotion.

They broke apart slowly. Their eyes met again.

Audra could barely breathe. Her last breath was stuck in her chest. Her blood virtually sang through her veins. But Dominic didn't say anything. He only stared at her.

Finally she realized that maybe words weren't necessary. They'd already told each other how they felt. He'd kissed her. If she were really part of his life, she wouldn't be thrown by a kiss. The situation would continue on normally.

"Do you want to help with Joshua's morning routine?"

He took a breath. "Sure. I'll dress him myself again."

He walked Joshua to the dressing table and Audra gathered his clothes.

He rolled the baby onto the changing table and leaned in so his face was close. "Hey, there, Joshua. You like this, don't you?"

The baby cooed and laughed, slapping Dominic's cheeks with his chubby fingers.

Dominic caught the baby's hands and kissed each palm. "Behave."

The baby laughed.

Audra's heart swelled again. They were so cute together, so perfect and now it seemed as if she might fit into the picture, too.

Occupied with the baby, Dominic said, "I'm sorry that I keep getting distracted from something I want to tell you."

Audra laughed and teasingly said, "Sorry?"

"Yeah. Every time I get distracted, I delay your stay here." He peered over his shoulder at her. "I've been trying to say that I'm very grateful for your help. I know this really put you out — put a strain on your already busy schedule."

"Hey, don't forget you paid me well, and helped the Wedding Belles keep a promise."

He laughed. "You think we're even?"

"Yes."

"That may be true, but I'm not going to hold you to the entire one-month deal."

"You're not?"

Finished dressing Joshua, Dominic lifted the baby from the changing table. "No. There aren't words enough to thank you. So I think letting you out of the deal early is the best way to show my gratitude."

Holding the baby, he walked over and stood in front of her. "We owe this to you," he said, indicating the peace and comfort between him and his little boy. "We'll never forget you."

With that he turned and began walking to the door. "You're free to go."

Audra stood frozen. Just when she was ready to stay — or date him — certainly not expecting to go — she was free.

She packed in less than an hour and went looking for Dominic but was told he and the baby were out in the yard again. Beaming, Mary Greene hugged her daughter, told her she was proud of her, thanked her and then also just sort of dismissed her.

Audra had never felt so awkward. Had she only been a servant to him? An employee?

She took a long breath, glancing around the huge, silent foyer at the luxury, and knew the truth. She had only been an employee to him. And this Cinderella had to get back to the real world.

Swallowing hard, she lifted her suitcase and walked out. No fanfare. No emotion. Just silence.

Returning from a business lunch on Monday afternoon, with his driver's attention on the back road they'd taken to Mark Makin's residence, Dominic relaxed on his seat. Though he wished they wouldn't, his thoughts drifted to Audra.

The CDs she'd had made filled a hole Dominic hadn't known how to cope with. But the gesture itself told him more about Audra than he could have ever learned in a thousand dates. She saw through all his facades to the heart of his problem. Though she couldn't fix it, she had found a solution. Dominic hadn't felt this good in years.

And he'd had to let her go.

That didn't seem right. Fair. Something. Until he thought of the situation from Audra's perspective. He couldn't offer her anything permanent. Until his own life settled down a bit he couldn't even think about finding his own Mabel Fortune. So from time to time he'd miss Audra. But he'd have to deal with it.

He took a breath and glanced out of the window at the beautiful landscape, realizing why Mark had built his estate this far out in the country and why he worked from his home office. The peace and tranquility of the area seemed to seep into Donminic's soul.

The road wound through farmland, occasionally disturbed by a small town, until the ratio of small towns to farms shifted. On the edge of the final town before Dominic's driver would have eased onto the highway into Boston, an enormous sign announced Gina's Italian Restaurant.

Normally the sign wouldn't have caught his attention, but taking in the scenery as he had been, he couldn't miss it. Just then he saw a car like Audra's in the parking lot. It wasn't the only gray car of that make he'd ever seen with a bright-red bumper sticker, but if the bumper sticker said Wedding Belles, then he pretty much figured Audra was in the restaurant.

On impulse, he leaned forward, tapped Jimmy's shoulder and said, "Pull in there."

As Jimmy maneuvered around the lot, he said, "Drive by that car. See if you can read the bumper sticker."

Jimmy laughed. "The bumper sticker?"

"It should say something about wedding planners —"

Jimmy's eyes narrowed as he looked ahead at the car Dominic thought was Audra's. "No wedding planners . . . Wedding Belles . . ."

"That's it," Dominic said with a laugh. "Drop me off at the door. I won't be long." He just wanted to say hello. Really. Just say hello and see her. Just for a minute.

"Yes, sir."

He couldn't imagine why she'd have lunch this late . . . or at a restaurant so far out of town. But here she was and he couldn't resist stopping.

He stepped out of his car and walked to the door. When he pushed it open, darkness greeted him. As his eyes adjusted, he saw neon lights advertising different brands of beer above a dimly lit wood bar, but the only light in the rest of the room came from candles on the center of tables covered with red-and-white checked tablecloths.

It was close to two o'clock in the afternoon. Lunch was over and dinnertime wasn't for a few hours, but the bar was packed. And the clientele didn't look the best in the world. Denim, leather vests and jackets, biker chains and boots dominated the room.

A roar of laughter erupted from the area beyond the bar, and Dominic saw three or four guys playing pool.

Ignoring that, he scanned the restaurant section, looking for Audra. It took a few scans before he found her, sitting at the last table in the corner of the otherwise empty dining room. Alone.

Alone? She'd come to an out-of-town restaurant alone? A restaurant that had this kind of crowd?

A short, bald man approached. A huge red apron covered his white shirt and black trousers. "Can I help you, sir?"

"Uh . . ." He couldn't remember the last time he'd been to a restaurant were the maître d' didn't know his name. Or the last time he'd gone to a restaurant without a reservation. Worse, he hadn't come here for food.

He pointed to the far corner where Audra sat. "Do you know that woman back there?"

He followed Dominic's line of vision and smiled. "Audra."

"Audra Greene?"

He nodded. "Yes."

"Can I sit with her?"

He laughed. "I'd say that's up to her." He grabbed a menu and led Dominic through the maze of tables, stopping at Audra's. Up close Dominic could see her laptop open at the place beside hers. Though there was a salad in front of her, her gaze was on the papers to her right.

As they approached, she glanced up. "Dominic?"

"Hey."

"What are you doing here?"

"I saw your car as I was driving by. Bumper sticker gives you away."

She winced. "I guess."

"A little advertising never hurt anyone." He pointed at the empty place. "Mind if I sit?"

She scrambled to gather her papers, but he stopped her. "Don't worry about it. I just want a cup of coffee —"

He turned to the man in the apron as he said that, and the man scurried away. Sitting on the chair across from her, he said, "What's up?"

She took a breath. "I'm working."

"This is Wedding Belles' office?"

"No, we're in a brownstone." She took another breath. "Julie does the bookkeeping for Wedding Belles and there really isn't enough other work for a full-time accountant, so I have additional clients on the side."

He glanced around. "Places like this?"

She tilted her head in question. "Gina's is a very popular restaurant."

"I can see it's popular, but I don't see anybody eating." His gaze paused meaningfully on the men playing pool.

"This used to be a biker bar. Every once in a while a group wanders in, expecting a different atmosphere."

He laughed.

She finally smiled. "Really, they're harmless. After a time or two of trying to shoot pool in a place that's playing Dean Martin's Italian love songs, they pretty much don't come back."

When the waiter returned with Dominic's coffee, Audra said, "Bring Mr. Manelli a plate of manicotti. Put it on my bill."

"Sure."

The waiter scampered away again.

"I've had lunch."

She shrugged. "So, you'll only have a bite to sample it. Then you'll understand why I think this restaurant is going to be Boston's next big thing."

"And you'll be the accountant for Boston's next big thing?"

She smiled. "Yeah. Nothing wrong with that. I like upstarts. People at the beginning of something big. Dreaming and then making those dreams come true."

He'd never heard that kind of excitement in her voice. "You like what you do?"

"Of course, I do." She toyed with her fork, then looked him in the eye. "Before I met David, I had a dream of someday becoming a CEO. Of running something really important. I think I forgot that."

"Oh?"

She took a breath. "Yeah. I was sort of trying to tell you this the other day in the nursery, but —"

"But I kissed you, then asked you to leave."

She nodded.

He sat back on his chair. "Huh."

Audra said nothing. *That* was as close as she would allow herself to come to telling him that she'd accept a date if he offered.

He looked around again, brought his gaze back to hers and said, "How does *this* fit into that plan?"

She laughed. "It's a very long road to get to the office on the top floor. So I'm creating my own. I've already started my own accounting firm." She shrugged. "Who knows? With enough clients like this — clients who expand — pretty soon I might be able to hire help."

She motioned in a circle. "Gina and Tony are already looking at a second location for Gina's in the city. They can do that because they built up a rental property business, long before they opened Gina's. Not just so they'd have capital to invest, but also to have money to live on." She smiled at him. "Someday, when you're looking for an investor, you may just be coming to them."

He glanced around. Audra's heart was in her throat. She couldn't be more plain if she spelled it out on a blackboard, yet he didn't seem to be getting it.

The waiter returned with the manicotti. "This is Tony, by the way. Tony, this is Dominic Manelli."

Dominic rose to shake his hand. "A pleasure to meet you."

"You, too." Tony bobbed his head. "Taste Gina's manicotti. See if that doesn't make you weep and thank your Maker."

Audra laughed gaily. Dominic glanced at her as he sat and then reached for his fork. He slid the pasta manicotti into his mouth and his eyes squeezed shut. "Oh, Lord."

Tony's chest puffed out with pride. "It's good, right?"

"It's the best food I've ever eaten."

Tony scampered away saying, "I'll tell Gina."

Audra laughed. "You better hope I don't tell Joyce . . . or my mother what you just said."

He tilted his head, studying her. "I can't believe the difference in you."

"What?" She plucked a cucumber from the salad beside her laptop and popped it into her mouth.

"You're . . . you're . . . sunny and focused and different. Businesslike but in a happy way."

She laughed. "Gina and Tony bring out the best in me."

"I can see that."

"This is the real me. The Audra I was

before David."

"And this Audra is happy?"

"Happy. Strong. Smart." Sucking in a breath for courage, she caught his gaze. "And not above having a little fun. Just going out to have fun. I used to like to have fun. I used to date to have fun. My mistake," she said, holding his gaze, "was thinking David would settle down."

To her surprise Dominic burst out laughing. He rose from his seat. "I told you so."

"Yes, you did, but a real gentleman doesn't say I told you so."

He caught her gaze again. This time his eyes turned serious, smoldering with heat. She knew exactly what he meant when he said, "I'm not always a gentleman, Audra."

She held his gaze. "No kidding."

"No kidding."

"I think, after almost three weeks of living with you, I know that. I know who you are."

He thought about that for a few seconds. Finally, he took a deep breath and said, "I have to get back to work."

She nodded.

He turned to walk away but turned again. "It was really nice to see you."

Disappointment fluttered through her. She couldn't have been more clear. And she

186

knew he'd understood. But he didn't want her.

"Yeah. Nice to see you, too."

With that he walked away, and Audra sank into her chair. She'd just made a fool of herself.

Chapter Ten

A week later, with the new nanny in place and no contact with Audra in seven long days, Dominic paced his huge office. He'd let the week go by to draw a clean line between their relationships. He didn't want her to think of herself as an employee. He did want her to think of herself as somebody he was so darned attracted to that he sometimes couldn't breathe in her presence. But he wanted a clear demarcation between their working relationship and their personal relationship.

He decided that would take about two weeks, but today he couldn't stop thinking about her, and today — if he called her and she agreed to go out with him — all this sexual-frustration and missing-her misery could be over.

He strode to his desk and grabbed the receiver of his phone as he fell into the tall-back chair. While assisting him with Joshua,

Audra had given him her cell phone number in case of an emergency and he dialed it from memory. She answered on the first ring.

At the sound of her voice he was suddenly tongue-tied and he said the first thing that popped into his head. "I thought you might want to know about things that have happened with Joshua."

"Dominic?"

The question in her voice caused his stomach to tighten. Was she forgetting him? "Yeah. I just thought — you know — you would want to hear about things with Joshua, so I thought I'd call and let you know he's getting a tooth."

"Oh." She laughed. "I'm sitting here thinking that's adorable, but I'll bet you're having some sleepless nights."

"Should I be ashamed to admit I'm not?"

She laughed again. "No. Not if you hired a nanny."

"I did."

"Then I'm sure that if the nanny can't soothe him back to sleep when he wakes, you've told her to come and get you."

Dominic settled more deeply, more comfortably into his chair. The sound of her voice, the very normal way she treated him, soothed him. "No. I didn't realize I should tell her that." He paused and then added. "I'm still not a pro with this baby stuff. What could I do to help her?"

"Having you hold him and comfort him might be enough."

"Oh, okay. I get it." He smiled. "So the kid loves me, huh?"

"Yep. There's no accounting for taste."

He burst out laughing, and his heart swelled. But the conversation had also died. It was his moment of truth. Take the risk that she wanted what he wanted. A simple, uncomplicated relationship. Or back away.

No decision had ever seemed so important. Or so difficult.

He heard the jingle of a phone in the background before Audra said, "That's my work phone. I gotta go."

He opened his mouth, but nothing came out. What if she said no? What if he insulted her by asking? He was so sure she'd been hinting the week before. What if he was wrong?

The phone on her end rang again.

"You know you can call me anytime you want."

"About Joshua?"

"About Joshua." She paused then said. "Or whatever."

He took a breath and decided to jump in

with both feet. "Or we could have dinner."

Another pause. The phone in her office rang again. Time stretched out as she obviously debated. Dominic squeezed his eyes shut. He'd put her in the horrible position of having to refuse him. She knew, just as he did, that they were worlds apart. And she probably didn't want the hassle of trying to fit into his.

"Okay."

His breathing restarted. *Okay?* "Tonight?"

"I —" She paused again. Dominic waited, breath stalled in his chest again. "Sure. Why not?"

"Okay. Tonight. I'll be by around seven."

He could hear the smile in her voice when she said, "Great."

When they hung up, he rose from his desk chair and headed out of his office. They might come from two different worlds, but it didn't matter. They weren't working toward anything permanent. He wanted a simple, uncomplicated relationship. Someone to have fun with. Someone to talk to.

And he could see from their conversation at the restaurant, that was what she wanted, too. He might have a business to run, but she had a business to *build.* She needed something uncomplicated as much as he did.

■ ■ ■ ■

The conversation through dinner was unlike any conversation they'd had before. Dominic talked about the work he had done that day and his plans for Manelli Holdings and how some things were working well while others weren't. Not only did Audra understand everything he discussed, but she had valuable input. Suddenly she saw everything he'd seen all along. Even though their lives were worlds apart, professionally they were now in the same boat. And personally they clicked.

A band began playing in the corner of the large room and Dominic led her to the dance floor. He pulled her close, nestling her against him, and every worry Audra had about their potential life together flew out of her head. She'd never been this attracted to anyone before. Not even David. This was the man she was made to be with. She refused to think any further than today. Being held in his arms, so close she could feel his breathing, knowing he wanted her — her — was amazing.

They danced two songs without breaking apart even when the music ended. But just as the third song was about to begin, he glanced back at their table and then grinned at her.

"I see Andre has brought out dessert."

She stepped close, wanting to dance again. "Not interested."

"Come on. Please." He pulled away, caught her hand and began dragging her toward their table. "I love cake."

"Hey, I like cake, too, but —"

The area was dark, and a quick glance told Audra that while they danced, the table had been cleared of their dinner dishes, and a small white cake sat in the center, surround by candles in little red votive cups.

"What's this?"

"Sit!" He pulled out her chair. "I have a little something for you."

She narrowed her eyes at him, but sat as he had ordered. He handed a little jewelers box to her. Not ring size. A little bigger. Big enough that she wouldn't get confused.

"A present?"

"Open it."

She flipped the lid on the small square box and gasped when she saw the heart-shaped charm on a gold chain. She glanced up at him. "It's beautiful."

"It's a locket." He nodded at the box. "Open it."

She pulled the necklace from the box and

opened the locket to find pictures of Dominic and Joshua.

"You helped me find my way back to sanity with some pictures. I thought I could use pictures to show you how I feel about you."

Connected. That was the first word that came to mind. Then family. He thought of her as family. A part of his life.

Her chest tightened. Butterflies took flight in her stomach. Happiness overwhelmed her. She loved him. He was good, kind, responsible, as perfect as the necklace he had given her. They were good for each other. They helped each other. And they were so attracted a mere kiss could melt her. She'd be a fool not to see what was going on between them. They were committing. They simply weren't using a ring or a piece of paper.

"Here," he said, removing the locket from the case and rising to walk behind her chair. He looped the chain around her neck and the heart fell with a soft plop on her chest.

He reached for her hand. "Let's go home."

Home. He'd said it that way because he knew she belonged with him, and now, with the locket, she did.

They spent the drive kissing in the backseat

of his car and entered the foyer, laughing, snuggling. Before they'd reached the steps, her mother walked into the hall from the door behind the huge curving stairway, holding Joshua.

Snuggled against Dominic, undoubtedly looking like A woman who had been thoroughly kissed, Audra felt like a child caught with her hand in the cookie jar. Her mother had seen her hundreds of times kissing David. Her mother also knew David had slept over at Audra's apartment and that she'd stayed in his mansion, sailed with him for weekends and gone on vacations with him. Her mother wouldn't condemn her for sleeping with someone.

But this was Dominic. Mary's employer. And, technically, Audra was the daughter of Dominic's hired help.

She casually straightened out of Dominic's hold.

"Mary?"

Her face and voice emotionless, Audra's mother said, "Your new nanny quit."

"Oh?"

"She tried to call you but didn't get an answer."

He winced. "I turned off my cell phone."

Mary smiled thinly, disapproval finally evident in her expression. Her gaze slid over to Audra, then immediately came back to Dominic.

"You have to be available when you have a baby."

Audra assumed the disapproval was meant for Dominic, a little scolding for turning off his phone. Nothing serious. Just enough that he would remember the lesson. But at the same time, Audra had been on the receiving end of her mother's gentle scolding one too many times to let herself off the hook so easily.

Her mother had warned her about dealing with Dominic. Even before Audra had decided to work for him, Mary had made sure Audra knew the youngest Manelli was a playboy. Then, when she and Dominic had had trouble communicating, Mary had reminded her daughter that Dominic was different. He'd been raised differently. Wanted different things. *Expected* different things. Played by different rules. Because he was wealthy. Privileged.

He took a breath. "You're right. I should have thought of that. But I —"

Had been so eager for our date that I forgot. Audra suspected that was what he had been about to say. And though the thought that he'd been as eager to see her as she had to see him filled her heart with even greater happiness than the locket he'd given her, it struck an odd chord with her. She wanted him to love her differently than he loved Joshua. Not more.

Joshua stretched from Mary's arms to Audra and Audra grabbed him. "Hey, sweetie." She brushed a kiss across his forehead as he snuggled into her chest.

Mary's mouth thinned again. "I'm not surprised he's cuddling you. I think he's missed you." She glanced back at Dominic again.

He smiled. "I get it. I'm the love giver. The one he's supposed to be accustomed to. The one he should reach for. I'll take him."

Audra handed him the baby, smiling with pride. He'd remembered the number-one lesson. The most important thing. Joshua was Dominic's family. He needed to give the love. So what if he forgot and turned off his cell phone? He was learning.

"Babies need two parents," Mary said, then she turned and walked back down the corridor, pushing through the swinging door before either Dominic or Audra had a chance to react.

Holding the squirming Joshua, Dominic took a breath. "I'm not sure what she meant by that."

But Audra knew. Her mother wouldn't condemn her for making love with someone. She considered that part of the process of finding a mate. But she knew Audra and Dominic had no intention of marrying. Though Audra considered that an outdated, antiquated way to look at life, her mother had actually made a better, stronger point. Dominic had no intention of marrying *her.* Audra knew that, but the ramifications of that hadn't sunk in until just this second. Someday Dominic would want to marry. And when he chose a wife, someone to help him raise Joshua, it wouldn't be her. She was the girl he was playing with.

She was the girl he was biding his time with.

He would never marry her.

And she knew better than to put herself in this kind of position. Her mother had raised her to fight for what she wanted, not settle for second place or second-rate, even if it did seem right in the moment.

Yet here she was, settling.

Dominic handed Joshua to her. "Here, you put him to bed. I'll grab a bottle of champagne and some chocolates and meet you in my room."

It didn't seem like an out-of-line request. She knew how to care for Joshua, and Dominic knew where to get the champagne. She didn't. Yet suddenly it all seemed wrong.

She licked her dry lips. "I, um, no."

Half-turned to the left, Dominic stopped. "No?"

"Didn't you hear what my mother said?"

"Yes." He frowned. "Which part?"

"A baby needs two parents."

"No, a baby needs family. Someone to love him. Not necessarily two people. Especially since I will always have a nanny to care for him."

"And I'm the nanny?"

"No."

But she stood there holding Joshua, had been told to put him to bed.

He ran his hand along the back of his neck. "I know this looks bad, but that's not how I see you."

"But you also don't see me as somebody you would marry."

"I'm not getting married."

"You say that now, but my mother was right. Eventually you're going to see that Joshua needs a mother. Once you get comfortable as overseer of Manelli holdings, you're going to realize you've settled down. And you're going to want someone to share your life with."

He stepped over and kissed her. "And who

says it won't be you?"

"You have." She plucked the locket from her throat. "This does." When he gave her a confused look she said, "We've known each other our entire lives. We've spent a good bit of the past few weeks together. I've fallen in love. You've fallen, too. But not in love. In lust. And this," she said, displaying the locket one more time, "is the best you can give me."

When he didn't reply, she drew in a shuddering breath as her eyes filled with tears. "In a way you're saying exactly what David said when he left me at the altar. I'm fun to have around, but I'm not a keeper."

She handed the baby to him, then reached behind her and removed the locket. Tears streaming down her cheeks, she gently placed the locket on his palm. "Goodbye, Dominic."

Head high, she walked out of the foyer. She prayed he'd come after her, and say all the right things to make her realize he did love her. But when she had enough time to call a cab company and have a car arrive to take her home, she knew he wasn't going to.

Dominic awakened the next morning feeling incredibly out of sorts. When he opened his eyes and saw his old bedroom, he had a flash of sensation that his life was good. That everything that had happened in the past months had been a dream. His parents weren't in Florida. Peter and Marsha were alive. His life was back to what it was supposed to be.

Then a soft cry issued from the baby monitor on his bedside table. He remembered he was sleeping in his old room because the nanny had left. He'd expected to come home with Audra, drink champagne and make love until dawn. Instead, because Mary met him and Audra at the door with Joshua, somehow his entire life had been turned upside down, and he'd spent a big part of the night calming a cranky baby.

He tried not to think of Audra pressing his locket into his palm before she walked out of his life. He could still feel the heat of the little gold heart, still feel the pain of rejection that sliced through him.

Joshua cried again.

He rolled out of bed, determined not to let this get to him. Peter's death had devastated him, nearly ruined him. He was finally getting himself back on track, understanding his place, loving Peter's son the way he should — the way he had to. Running the company as himself, not second-guessing what Peter would do. He couldn't let Audra's rejection take him down. Joshua needed him.

He entered the nursery, pajama bottoms low on his hips, rubbing the sleep from his eyes. "Hey, buddy."

Joshua sniffled at him.

He reached into the crib and pulled out the sobbing baby. But instead of Joshua's crying stopping, the little boy stretched around him as if looking for something — or someone.

He'd done it every day the first week Audra had been gone, and Dominic was smart enough to figure out that after seeing Audra last night, he was looking for her again today. That was why he'd jumped into her arms from Mary's the night before. He had missed Audra.

"She's not coming back." Saying the words caused a tsunami of disappointment to flood Dominic's chest, but he squelched it. How could he be upset when he didn't even understand what he'd done? They'd talked about having a relationship, but she'd somehow jumped them the whole way to marriage. He'd thought she understood what he wanted. But seeing her mother had changed everything.

He snorted a laugh. That was Mary. Strong enough that she barely had to say two words to get her point across. She didn't want him with her precious daughter. He got it.

"But we're okay. We can do this. We're family."

He changed the baby's diaper and took him downstairs to Joyce. "I understand the drill is that you watch him while I dress?"

Surprised, Joyce reached for Joshua. "It's the joy of my day," she said with a laugh. "But where's the nanny?"

"She quit. Mary was caring for him last night when I got back from dinner."

"Maybe we should call Audra?"

"Audra is gone and we're not bringing her back."

With that he turned and walked out of the room to the master suite, pretending nothing was wrong. He canceled his work schedule so that he and Mary could again interview nannies, and by the end of the day the tension in the room was so thick he couldn't take it anymore.

"Go ahead," he said, leaning back on the office chair in the den. "I know you want to ask."

"It's not my business."

"Normally I would agree, but since this

involves your daughter, we're in a different situation."

"Okay, then I'll ask. What's going on between the two of you?"

"Nothing. After you met us at the door with the baby, she left because she said she knew I would never marry her."

Mary smiled. "And apparently you let her leave because you have no intention of marrying her."

"I have no intention of marrying anyone."

"Then everything is the way it should be." Mary rose from her seat. "Dominic, you and my daughter aren't good for each other. You think she's a tough cookie and in some ways she is. But she's already had one heartbreak. She doesn't need another."

"I wouldn't have broken her heart."

Walking to the door, Mary said, "Of course you would. Not intentionally. But the second someone came along who suited your fancy more, you would have moved on. Unthinking. And Audra would have been standing as alone and vulnerable as she was at the back of that church waiting for David."

"I don't think anybody better than Audra could come along. There is no one better."

Mary laughed and turned to face him. "If you believe that, you should marry her. But you don't believe that. So leave it alone. Leave *her* alone."

When she was gone, Dominic tossed his pencil to his desk. If he didn't believe that, why did his heart hurt so much?

And if he did believe there was no one better than Audra, why couldn't he say he loved her? Why couldn't he see himself settling down with her? Marrying her? Growing old with her?

At ten-thirty that night, Audra grabbed a tissue from her desk and blew her nose, just as Belle walked in.

"What are you doing working! It's ten-thirty on a Saturday night!" She began, but her scolding tone stopped abruptly when she took a good look at Audra. "Audra?"

Audra looked up. Her eyes red. Her nose running. "I can't go home."

Belle rushed into the room. "Oh, sugar! What happened?"

"Everything was going really well with me and Dominic. We actually had a date last night. But when we got back to his house, my mother was there with the baby . . . and everything got screwed up. I suddenly felt like I was settling, or he was using me and my mother is his household manager, so it just seemed like he was only playing with

205

the hired help." She tossed her hands in despair. "He's never been in my apartment, but for some stupid reason or another every darn thing everywhere reminds me of him —"

"Honey, you are making absolutely no sense, but it doesn't matter. The beauty of me living next door is that I can whisk you away to my quarters and take care of you."

"Don't whisk me away!"

"Okay, honey," Belle said, leading her out of her office and to the small corridor that led to her apartment. "Nobody here wants to whisk you away. We need you."

After Belle encouraged Audra to drink a cup of chamomile tea, she directed her to the guest suite of her townhouse and told her to shower. When Audra was done, Belle returned with a pair of her pajamas. "They'll be big, but you'll be comfortable."

Wrapped in a towel, Audra took the pajamas. "Thanks, Belle."

"And tomorrow we're calling a meeting, and the girls and I can help you through this."

"No!"

Belle started. "No?"

Audra turned her back so she could slide into the pajama tops. "Could we keep this heartbreak a secret?"

"I don't see how you can."

She took a breath, stepping into the pajama bottoms. "I already hinted to Julie that I intended to take a tropical vacation. A few days away should be enough that I won't be crying when I return."

"But everybody —"

Audra pulled back the covers on the bed. "Please, Belle. One public humiliation was enough. Let me do this one in secret."

"Okay." She tucked Audra in. "I'll call my travel agent and get you a ticket. Where do you want to go?"

"Anywhere. And I've got an even bigger favor to ask you . . . could you call my mum? She'll explain."

The Sunday morning with Joshua was a total disaster. The moment the temporary nanny, whom Mary had somehow magicked out of thin air, picked up the baby, he didn't just cry; he screamed. After the first fifteen minutes, Dominic couldn't take it anymore. He forgot all about his pride and dialed Audra's cell phone number, ready to humble himself. But his call immediately went to voice mail. He tried at least twenty times before noon, but every time his call went to voice mail.

Furious, he left the nanny alone with

Joshua and strode into the kitchen. Mary and Joyce were going over menus. "Your daughter's not taking my calls."

Just then Mary's cell phone pinged. She grabbed her phone from her dress pocket. "Text message from Audra." She frowned. "It's one of those auto things that must be going to a lot of people." Her frown deepened. "She's going out of town. To St. Thomas?"

"Great. My son is sobbing for her, and she's going to play swimsuit model in the tropics."

He stormed out of the room and back to the nursery. To his surprise Joshua was sleeping soundly. Belle, the sixty-something Southern-belle temporary nanny, smiled. "I have a way with babies."

"Right. Or maybe he just settled down because I left the room." He ran his hand along the back of his neck.

"Don't think like that, sugar. He's just cranky this morning, and I managed to get him to sleep. So why don't you just go get some work done. I'm fine here."

He sucked in a breath. "Okay."

He left the nursery and walked to the den, where he intended to make a few calls, but as soon as he stepped into the room, he thought of Audra, because it was in this room that he'd planned their big dinner date.

He hadn't staffed it out as he usually did. No. He'd planned it himself. Every damned detail — for all the good it had done him.

He frowned. He hadn't done it for himself. Or to make points. He'd done it for her. He'd wanted to make her happy.

For all the good *that* had done him.

His frown deepened. Why did he keep doing that? Relating everything back to himself? He'd wanted to make Audra happy for her. Not for himself. He wasn't selfish when it came to her. Not really. He liked having her around, but he also loved pleasing her. It always seemed to him that nobody ever went out of their way to please her. But to him, buying her things, teasing her, including her in his life had been fun. Even the smallest gesture had been a wonderful surprise to her.

She had been very easy to please. Except for one big thing. She wanted him to marry her. And he didn't want to marry anybody.

The events of Monday morning were pretty much the same as Sunday's. Joshua awoke screaming. Dominic and Belle soothed the baby somewhat but not completely. One of them had to pace the floor with him all morning.

When Joshua finally lay down for a nap, Belle also decided to take a nap, and Dominic went to his den to work.

When he finished, he returned to the nursery. Joshua, though not screaming, was still fussy despite being with cuddly Belle, who appeared to be the kind of person who could charm birds from the trees. Still, her magic wasn't working on Joshua that morning.

"I have an idea," Dominic said, taking the baby from Belle. "The first nanny we had —" Merely thinking of Audra made his throat close. Yesterday he'd been angry, today he was sad. He missed Audra so damned much he couldn't even say her name, couldn't think about her without an avalanche of misery falling on him. "Anyway, she had a CD made of Joshua's parents." Though he knew Joshua missed Audra, Dominic also realized it was counterproductive to bring her back to soothe him. She wouldn't be in Joshua's life permanently. When she returned from the tropics, if he coerced her into visiting to spend time with the baby, Joshua would go through withdrawal again.

And so would he.

"I'm going to take him to the entertainment room and let his parents soothe him."

Belle smiled warmly. "That's a great idea."

Dominic headed for the door, but he stopped suddenly. "You wouldn't happen to want this job permanently would you?"

"I sort of have a full-time job. I'm just here to help a friend."

"But it's Tuesday."

Belle laughed. "I have a very flexible employer, so I can do this."

"Story of my life. Am I ever going to find a nanny who actually wants the job?"

He walked the baby to the entertainment room and, still holding Joshua, rifled through the CDs one-handed. Finally he found one they hadn't viewed the week before and he popped it into the CD drive.

Peter and Marsha suddenly appeared on the large screen. Dominic took a seat, settling Joshua on his lap. As soon as they sat, Joshua began to fuss.

"Shh. Look. There's your mom and dad."

Joshua screeched his unhappiness.

"Just give it a chance," Dominic said, growing impatient. Having control of nothing in his life was beginning to wear on him. He could think of a thousand women who would kill to go out with him while the one woman he wanted to be with didn't want to go out with him. Why? Because he wouldn't marry her. They hardly knew each other. Hadn't really dated. Hadn't slept together. Yet he was supposed to know he wanted to marry her?

It made no sense.

"Happy anniversary —" Peter's singsong voice drifted into the room.

Dressed in a pair of casual shorts and a sloppy T-shirt, Marsha turned to face Peter. "Happy anniversary? Anniversary of what?"

"We've been dating three weeks now."

Dominic lowered his forehead to his palm. Good God, his brother really had been a sap. Dominic was just about to stand to switch CDs, when Joshua began to giggle. This time when he screeched, it was a happy screech.

"Oh, you like that, huh?"

Joshua laughed.

"Come on, Marsha. Open your gift."

Marsha sighed. Dominic laughed. He'd never realized it before but Marsha was a lot like Audra. Prim and proper and logical. Peter had been the first guy to really get her to come out of her shell. He'd romanced her until she had become accustomed to having him around and she'd stopped thinking so much.

Dominic snorted a laugh. He'd tried romancing Audra, but though she'd loved the pajamas he'd bought her, she hadn't loved their romantic dinner.

He frowned. That wasn't true, either. That night had been perfect. She'd been so darned happy. And, if he remembered correctly, she hadn't wanted to leave the dance floor. She'd wanted to say in his arms.

She'd wanted to stay in his arms.

As Joshua giggled at the people on the screen, Dominic closed his eyes for a second and savored the memory of just holding Audra. He remembered feeling as if there was nobody else in the world. He remembered how happy he'd been.

Eyes closed, he let himself savor the memory, because he wasn't sure he'd ever feel that way about anyone else again.

His eyes popped open.

He couldn't see himself feeling this way about anybody again because he *wouldn't* feel that way about anyone else again!

CHAPTER ELEVEN

The next morning Dominic walked up to the door of the townhouse for Wedding Belles. The April sun warmed him, but that didn't help the jittery feeling in his stomach. He took a breath. He had to do this.

He opened the door, and a bright-eyed, strawberry-blonde greeted him. "Welcome to Wedding Belles," she said as if she were surprised to see him. "I take it you're someone's groom?"

He swallowed. "No. I'm here to see Audra Greene."

"Oh, my gosh! You're one of those nasty IRS people she's so terrified of, aren't you?"

Dominic laughed. "No."

Another blonde came barreling into the small foyer — which Dominic now realized served as the reception area for the business. Holding a huge bouquet of flowers, she blew her bangs out of her eyes.

"Julie, I . . ." Noticing Dominic, she

paused. "Who is this?"

"Someone to see Audra."

The blonde smiled craftily. "Oh, really." She stretched out her hand. "I'm Callie. Audra's best friend. What can I do for you?"

"Is she here?"

"Yes."

"Then you can show me to her office."

Callie's smile widened. "My pleasure."

From the eager expression on her face, Dominic expected to be grilled as they walked down the hall and up a long stairway. But she didn't say a word — though a woman with pins in her mouth and another holding a cake peered out of open doors as if he were a specimen on exhibit.

Enormously relieved when he and Callie stopped at a closed door, Dominic blew his breath out on a sigh.

Callie laughed. "I don't know who you are. I don't know what's going on between you and Audra, but good luck. She's in a mood."

And he was at fault.

And he was potentially about to make things worse.

"I don't know how anybody can come back from the tropics angry, but somehow our Audra managed it." Callie opened the door.

Framed by butter-yellow curtains, Audra sat behind a huge desk that dominated the room. When she saw him, her eyes widened with pleasure, but that expression was quickly replaced by wariness.

"What do you want?"

"I need to talk to you."

"I think we've said everything we had to say to each other at your house the other night."

"At the time so did I. But being without you hasn't been easy. Joshua —"

Her expression changed to one of fear. "Is Joshua okay?"

"He's fine, but —"

"But you don't want to have to spend so much time with him." The disappointment in her voice cut to Dominic's heart and angered him.

"You knew I was turning into a very good father when you left. Nothing's changed."

Audra sagged with relief. "I'm glad."

Expecting an argument, Dominic was at a loss for words. For a few seconds silence reigned.

Audra took a long, deep breath. "So why are you here?"

For all the planning Dominic had done in the car, words failed him. His heart hurt. He was tired. But more than that, he felt empty. How did a person explain that to someone whom he'd hurt? Why should she care?

He glanced at Callie. "Any possibility we can have some privacy?"

"Hey, Audra may think we're all oblivious to her because her work doesn't interact with ours, but we've all seen that she had another broken heart. If you're here to hurt her, I'm not going to stand for it. I'm probably going to sock you."

Dominic couldn't help it; he laughed. Audra bristled. "Callie, I can fight my own battles."

Dominic knew that for a fact. "Trust me. She holds her own with me." He turned and caught Audra's gaze. "And it's not my intention to hurt her."

Audra faced Callie. "Give us a minute."

"But —"

"Out."

Callie huffed a breath and marched to the door.

Audra said, "Close that behind you."

Callie huffed again, but closed the door as she left.

Audra decided not to say a word. He'd broken her heart, worse than David had. Her pain after being left at the altar had more to do with humiliation than missing

David. Dominic's heartbreak had been private, so her tears were from the loss of *him.* His love. Everything they could have been together. She didn't think it was possible for a body and soul to ache, but hers had. Now he was here. Looking breathtakingly handsome. Strong. Smart. Capable. Cute. She couldn't fault herself for falling for him — except she'd known better. Yet she'd followed him one step at a time until she was so in love with him that it was a physical feeling. Then he'd brought her crashing back to earth, and once again she was picking up the pieces of her life because another man might like her, might see the benefit of having her around, but he didn't love her.

And as illogical as it was — because she wasn't even entirely sure it existed anymore — she wanted that total, all-encompassing devotion. She wanted somebody to love her.

"I came to tell you that I am sorry."

"Sorry?"

"I know I hurt you —"

"Don't worry about it. I'm an adult who knew exactly the kind of man you are. You have nothing to be sorry for."

He rubbed his hand across the back of his neck. "Audra, everything in life doesn't boil down to simple logic."

"Really?"

He laughed. "Really."

"So you're here for something illogical?"

"Actually, yes." He took a few steps further into her office. "I'm here to ask you to marry me."

Damn it. She should have expected this. He wasn't the kind of guy to let a woman reject him. He was so accustomed to getting his own way he probably believed proposing was the right thing to do — at least for the moment. Once his panic over being left had disappeared, then he could reject her.

"No."

"No?"

"Come on, Dominic. You're just angry that I rejected you. So you're offering me what I told you I wanted. Marriage. But you don't want to marry me. For all practical intents and purposes I'm the maid's daughter."

"Is that what this is all about?"

"Isn't it?"

"No! Audra, I genuinely believed I wouldn't ever want to marry anybody."

"Oh, I get it. What my mother said has sunk in. You realize you do need a mother for Joshua. I'm the logical choice." She shook her head in misery. "But I don't want that, either." It hurt to remember their last argument, and the way he let her go, not even calling after her as she left his foyer. There was no way she'd start this again.

"Okay. I must be doing this all wrong, because this time I *know* we want the same thing." He paused, closed his eyes.

"The house is empty without you." He opened his eyes and caught her gaze again. "I feel like half a person. I get up every day with the realization that this day is going to go on just like every other day before it. That the sun will come out but it won't make any difference. I can have anything that I want, anytime I want it, but it won't matter."

He drew in a breath and walked a little closer to her desk. "Some days I wake up so empty, I swear it's a physical pain."

She knew the feeling very well. She'd lived it for months after David and was now experiencing an even worse version because she loved Dominic a hundred times more than she'd ever loved David.

"Sounds like depression," she said, rising from her seat so she could show him to the door. "I'd suggest you call your doctor."

"There's no reason to call a doctor. I've figured out what was wrong."

"Well, your doctor's the only one who can

prescribe antidepressants." She rounded her desk. "I can't help you with that."

He caught her arm and stopped her. "I don't want a doctor. I don't need anti-depressants. I just need to get you back into my life."

"I already figured out that's why you're asking me to marry you. I rejected you because you told me you would never marry me, so now —"

"Audra, I love you."

For a few seconds the world stopped spinning. Time suspended. Still, those words *could* only be part of his ploy not to be rejected by her. "Nice try."

"Not really. So far loving you has only made me miserable. But I can't seem to change the fact that I do love you." He laughed. "You are perfect — almost as if you were made for me to love. You laugh at my jokes, don't let me be less than the man I can be, and you love me, too." Holding her gaze, he said, "You said it Friday. I dismissed it as meaningless. But nothing you say is meaningless. You love me. And I love you. And even though I have no idea how to make a marriage work, I also had no idea how to raise a baby, yet I caught on. So, seeing as how we'll already start off loving each other, I'd say spending the rest of our lives together should be easy."

She didn't say anything, simply stared at him, hoping against hope that he meant the things he was saying.

"I now understand Peter and Marsha. Why they didn't want to be apart. Why they took three million pictures of every darned thing they did together. They could have been the two poorest people in the world and they would have been happy. Because they had each other."

"You don't care that I'm your house manager's daughter?"

He laughed. "Only that she'd skin me alive if I hurt you." He took a step closer and caught her arms. "What I feel for you has nothing to do with who your mother is. Nothing to do with Joshua. It has nothing to do with losing my old life or taking over Peter's. I finally realized you would have changed my world all by yourself."

"Really?" Her voice was soft, vulnerable and desperate. Even she heard it. She wanted to believe him so badly that she prayed she wasn't misinterpreting him.

He smiled. "Really."

"You love me?"

He chuckled. "I love you."

"Forever?"

"Forever . . . and with all the accompanying mushiness. Watching one of the CDs you made for Joshua caused me to see that I felt about you the way Peter felt about Marsha, but I hadn't said it very well. Because I was totally out of my element. Facing something I not only never thought I'd face, but something I didn't think I wanted. I honestly didn't believe I was the kind of guy to marry anybody. But I want to marry you and it scares me."

She laughed.

"I think you're the most beautiful, most wonderful, most maddening person in the world. But that last part is what I know will keep us from getting bored."

She laughed.

"So do you want to tell the friends who are listening at the door that they have another wedding to plan?"

"Yes and no."

"Yes and no?"

"The last wedding I had sort of left me with a bad taste in my mouth for standing at the back of a church in a wedding gown." She sucked in a breath. "I'd like to go to a justice of the peace and then take off for somewhere tropical."

"You just were someplace tropical."

"And I sat around thinking of you the whole time. So now it would be nice to actually be there with you."

"After three months of being overwhelmed with work, two weeks on an island sounds like heaven."

"You're the boss."

He laughed. "Nah. No bosses here. I like us better as a team."

She smiled. "So do I."

Then he kissed her, long and deep, connecting their lives, entwining their destinies. He didn't have to say the words. She didn't need to hear them. His kiss and the way her body responded to it said it all.

Susan tells us all about the unexpected twist to her own big day:

"The day of my wedding, a blizzard pounded our side of the state. Only about half the expected guests showed up and they were rowdy — if only because they were thrilled to be out of the storm. After the bridal dance, my aunt took my shoe for luck. So when our car slid off the icy roads and got stuck in a snowdrift on the drive home, we couldn't walk. I only had one shoe.

Eventually, a good Samaritan stopped to help — and he just happened to be one of my former bosses. He gave us a ride to a gas station, and the attendant and my husband took the tow truck to get our car. I walked into the garage in my wedding gown with one bare foot, not sure how long I'd have to wait or explain to customers why I was partially shoeless.

My husband and I were so tired when we got home that we ended up playing gin rummy most of the night. It seemed like a horrible way to start a marriage, but considering that the marriage has been filled with love and laughter, it must not have been. Standing in the garage with one shoe, I never realized I'd come to love that story.

Plus, when anybody wants to talk about weddings, I have the best story!"

Catch up with Susan and her latest projects at www.susanmeier.com.

Visit www.harlequin-thewedding planners.blogspot.com to find out more. . .

We hope you have enjoyed this Large Print book. Other Thorndike, Wheeler, and Chivers Press Large Print books are available at your library or directly from the publishers.

For information about current and upcoming titles, please call or write, without obligation, to:

Publisher
Thorndike Press
295 Kennedy Memorial Drive
Waterville, ME 04901
Tel. (800) 223-1244

or visit our Web site at:

http://gale.cengage.com/thorndike

OR

Chivers Large Print
published by BBC Audiobooks Ltd
St James House, The Square
Lower Bristol Road
Bath BA2 3SB
England
Tel. +44(0) 800 136919
email: bbcaudiobooks@bbc.co.uk
www.bbcaudiobooks.co.uk

All our Large Print titles are designed for easy reading, and all our books are made to last.